W9-AEV-745

Dr. Frankenstein's Daughters

ALSO BY SUZANNE WEYN

The Bar Code Tattoo

The Bar Code Rebellion

The Bar Code Prophecy

Reincarnation

Distant Waves: A Novel of the Titanic

Empty

Invisible World: A Novel of the Salem Witch Trials

DR. FRANKENSTEIN'S DAUGHTERS

SUZANNE WEYN

Scholastic Press ● *New York*

Library of Congress Cataloging-in-Publication Data

Weyn, Suzanne.
Dr. Frankenstein's daughters / by Suzanne Weyn. — 1st ed.
p. cm.
Summary: Giselle and Ingrid are the twin daughters of Doctor Victor Frankenstein, but they are very different people, and when they inherit his castle in the Orkney Islands, Giselle dreams of holding parties and inviting society — but Ingrid is fascinated by her father's forbidden experiments.
ISBN 978-0-545-42533-9 (hardcover)
1. Frankenstein, Victor (Fictitious character) — Juvenile fiction. 2. Human experimentation in medicine — Juvenile fiction. 3. Monsters — Juvenile fiction. 4. Twins — Juvenile fiction.
5. Sisters — Juvenile fiction. 6. Diaries — Juvenile fiction. 7. Horror tales. 8. Orkney (Scotland) — Juvenile fiction. 9. Diary fiction. [1. Horror stories. 2. Mystery and detective stories. 3. Monsters — Fiction. 4. Human experimentation in medicine — Fiction.
5. Twins — Fiction. 6. Sisters — Fiction. 7. Diaries — Fiction. 8. Orkney (Scotland) — Fiction.] I. Title. II. Title: Doctor Frankenstein's daughters.
PZ7.W539Dq 2013
813.54 — dc23
2012033039

10 9 8 7 6 5 4 3 2 1   13 14 15 16 17

Printed in the U.S.A.   23
First edition, January 2013

The text type was set in Mrs Eaves.
Book design by Elizabeth B. Parisi

FOR DAD AND MOM, TED AND JACKIE WEYN.

With thanks to the editorial team of David Levithan (of course, always), Erin Black, and Annie McDonnell (thanks to you both for your care and thoroughness). Thanks too to Bill Gonzalez for talking this story through with me and all your suggestions.

PROLOGUE

FROM THE PERSONAL DIARY OF

VICTOR FRANKENSTEIN

Ingolstadt, Germany

June 15, 1798

What unbearable guilt! I am the most wretched man alive — a blasted tree, shattered. I am abhorrent to even myself.

My gentle and good wife, Hildy, dead. Only nineteen years of age and already gone from my arms, defeated in her struggle to give birth to our sweet tiny girls, Giselle and Ingrid. I imagine them blooming into beauties, reproducing Hildy's luscious dark hair, violet eyes, and avid intellect. But this I shall never witness myself. In years to come they may well curse my name, but I am compelled to abandon my daughters, and pray that they do not suffer too greatly. To claim them as my own would be to endanger their very existence. Who knows what this fiend I have created is capable of?

Tonight, by moonlight, I will head toward the Swiss mountains with the intent of drawing the Monster away from Ingolstadt, and thereby keep him from learning that this night I have become the father of twin girls.

For two long years the fiend has hounded me. I thought I could keep ahead of him but it is no use. He finally caught up with me on the slopes of Mount Montanvert and took me to his wretched hovel. He told me of his life these last years and I was amazed at how he had educated himself and yet grown so cold and hard in his emotional state. In that hovel, he presented his demand: "Make me a mate or I will destroy you."

I shuddered at the hideousness of his request but he added a threat to ensure my cooperation. "I will work at your destruction, nor finish until I have desolated your heart, so that you shall curse the hour of your birth." This he swore to do if I would not promise to make him a bride. To prove he was capable of such fiendishness, the Monster revealed it was he who had killed my younger brother, William, just as I had suspected.

I was right to fear his wrath and move as far away from my precious twin daughters as possible. How happy I am that he does not know of their existence.

March 15, 1801

I have arrived this week by boat to Castle Frankenstein, left to me by my mother, Caroline Beaufort Frankenstein, who was a relative of its previous owner. The castle is believed to be built by the fierce Viking conqueror Sweyn. It is massive, and with its decaying stone walls, it appears to be one of this small, rugged island's oldest structures.

I have avoided the Monster's request lo these many months as I studied to make an improvement on the form of this new female creature, but the time has finally come to comply, lest the fiend grow impatient and unleash the murderous spree he has sworn to undertake.

This castle will be the ideal location for a laboratory and especially suited to my pursuits because a secret underground tunnel of ingenious engineering connects it to an even smaller, more deserted island — a most tantalizing discovery!

The other day I followed the tunnel through a cavernous underground space, and from there was able to scale the rock wall that opened into a meager hut on the oversized rock they call Sweyn Holm, that overlooks a crashing ocean. I knew immediately that I had found the perfect site for my purposes — the construction of a female companion as demanded by the Monster, who dogs my every step. This is the promise he has extracted from me. In exchange he vows to retreat with his companion to South America, never to threaten me or those I love again.

The sooner I embark on this unholy travesty, the more quickly I can return to reclaim my girls. I am told they are now living with Hildy's widowed father, the Baron Von der Wien, in Ingolstadt. I will convince him that I can provide Ingrid and Giselle with a wonderful life once the Monster has left. I will even wed again to provide them with a stepmother. There is nothing I will not do for my daughters.

April 8, 1801

I am immersed in solitude and miserable beyond utterance. The female I have built is an exquisite creature with abundant black hair and a radiant complexion, graceful in form and visage. Yet when I look upon her — her curls tossed over the end of the table, her eyelids shimmering over their sockets as though at any moment they will open to reveal sparkling orbs — it is not pride but engulfing shame that consumes me.

How could I have not seen it until this very moment? But without doubt it is so.

I have, without conscious intent, re-created my Hildy! I have built a bride not for the Monster, but for myself!

Only now do I shed the tears I was too frantic to cry when I first learned of Hildy's death.

I feel the Creature out there, lurking. I have felt him there in the periphery of my life from the moment I created him six years ago, when I was merely a lad of nineteen. The Monster has shadowed me throughout this trip and I know now he is still near — closer than ever — awaiting his bride.

I will not give him my Hildy!

Before I let him love my darling, I will destroy her. She is my greatest achievement and yet I must exterminate her. My eyes blinded by hot tears, I raise my surgeon's hacksaw to annihilate this assemblage of organs, nerve, and flesh before I am tempted to bring it to life and love it utterly.

April 10, 1801

The Monster is in a rage! He now knows I have broken my vow to build him a companion. I have hacked his would-be wife into pieces and thrown them into the wild Irish Sea.

The Monster has once more sworn vengeance on all I love, this time with renewed and terrible commitment.

My dear friend Henry Clerval has already been murdered. I must race back to Geneva to do what I can to protect my family. I only thank the gods that I never claimed my two baby daughters. No one knows they are connected to me, and thus they remain safe.

May God bless them and keep them so always.

CHAPTER ONE

Pavia, Lombardy, Italy
May 17, 1815

Dearest Giselle,

How I miss you! I knew it would not be easy to part with my dear twin, and my heart aches to see you again. Studying here with Count Volta has been fascinating, beyond my wildest dreams. I am still amazed that Grandfather agreed to have this scientific genius tutor me. I suppose he knew I was going mad with boredom there in Ingolstadt and needed some outlet for my restless mind.

It is quite agreeable here. Aunt Gertrude's apartment over the piazza is enchanting. Though she is not overly strict, she stays in listening distance when I entertain Anthony Verde, a young man I have met here. He is quite good-looking but speaks no German. Since my Italian is only adequate, we converse in English. Our relationship is one of friendship and not romance, but it is lovely to have a friend when so far from home.

But allow me to get to the true purpose of this letter. It is quite astonishing, as you will soon learn.

The other day a man came to Aunt Gertrude's apartment and introduced himself as Baron Ernest Frankenstein.

The name meant nothing to me, but Aunt Gertrude blanched deadly white the moment he spoke it. Indeed, she staggered backward dramatically. If I hadn't steadied her by the elbow, I think she might have fallen over.

I too was dizzied by Baron Frankenstein's next revelation: He claimed to be the brother of our mysterious father!

Apparently our disgraced father was a doctor named Victor Frankenstein. He married our mother while a student at the University of Ingolstadt but disappeared without explanation on the very night of our births. Now Ernest Frankenstein says he has recently learned that Victor Frankenstein died some time ago in the Arctic Circle, a complete lunatic. For years no one knew if he was dead or alive, but in recent months the arrival in Germany of his frozen corpse (encased in a block of ice!) confirmed his death beyond doubt.

It is a lot to comprehend. I am sure you yourself are dizzy with such a flood of information after so many years of drought. To find our father — and then lose him in practically the same breath. It is hard to know how to mourn.

And that is not all. You and I, dear sister, have quite suddenly become wealthy, independent women. In addition to a monetary inheritance from our father, we are now the owners of a castle on one of the rugged, rocky islands to the north of Scotland. It is in an island chain known as the Orkneys.

Life can change in an instant, sister. Ours has.

Aunt Gertrude has taken it upon herself to write to Grandfather, informing him of the news and its details. She has also sent him a copy of the legal documents involved. But I wanted to write to you first.

I am not sure yet how I want to deal with this sudden development. It can't be a bad thing to now have financial resources of our own. If nothing else, it frees us from having to marry one of Grandfather's "eligible" old bachelors to secure our future.

I must run off to sleep. Because even as my head swirls with all of these new developments, the old life continues. Tomorrow we will be visited by the Englishman William Nicholson. I am most interested to learn his ideas on electrolysis, a fancy term for the decomposition of water into hydrogen and oxygen by the use of voltaic current. (Named for my amazing Count Volta, of course!)

I miss you madly. Write and let me know what you think of all this.

I remain your loving twin,

Ingrid

CHAPTER TWO

FROM THE DIARY OF

GISELLE VON DER WIEN

June 7, 1815

What an exhausting journey this has been and how relieved I am that it is finally coming to an end. Let my foolish, ignorant decisions stay back in the past, where they belong. There is no returning to Ingolstadt now that I have made my decision regarding our father's inheritance and angered our grandfather so greatly. My humiliating behavior over Johann can now be buried forever under the ground of this new life. Daunting as this new venture may be, it is better to forget and be happy.

Soon I will see Ingrid again and meet this mysterious Baron Frankenstein on the isle of Gairsay in Orkney. I am dying to view the castle that has fallen to us by way of our inheritance from our enigmatic father.

This morning when I arrived in Kirkwall, the largest city in the biggest of the island chain, I was eager to continue on to the much less inhabited island of Gairsay, where Castle Frankenstein is located, but was informed that the sea was too wild to afford a safe crossing. And so, I had to wait until late in the afternoon today.

The captain of the small skiff I hired for the crossing is a man in his fifties named Captain Ramsay. He speaks little. His weather-beaten visage looks like it has never smiled and disapproves of all it sees.

Thankfully I have you, Diary, to write in, otherwise I would now be face-to-face with this taciturn captain as he steers this two-sailed craft, laden with the supplies he is bringing to the island. I am his only passenger.

This long journey has been an adventure in itself, as a female traveling alone attracts every sort of attention. I have learned to keep my head down, my eyes averted, and the brim of my bonnet decidedly forward so as not to make contact with strange men. A mere glance can invite all manner of unwanted conversation. I am grateful that I am nearing my destination and will once again be with my sister.

I don't like the way this man, the captain, keeps looking at me. Perhaps I was foolish to get into a boat with a man I don't know, but he had a for-hire sign up and it seemed reputable enough. I'm probably worrying over nothing and will not look at him. I will occupy myself with my writing.

As we sail past the small islands I see that the landscape here is largely untamed, with high rocky cliffs overlooking crashing shores and green fields dotted with thatched cottages. I am over-heated in my long navy-blue high-waisted coat and gray fur hat. My hand muff sits at my side. I assumed a chain of islands north of Scotland and not far from Scandinavia would be cold, even though it is spring, but I was wrong; we are treated to a balmy breeze, which I am told is thanks to the largess of the Gulf Stream. The weather is unusually temperate. In fact, I will break my writing here to divest myself of these heavy garments.

June 7 (continued)

I am back, feeling much better with only my Indian-design shawl over my brocade dress. My bonnet became impossible to keep on in the misty ocean spray and wind. My hair is fast coming undone, but I don't mind. In fact, this coming apart makes me feel newly set free from my old, mundane life back in Germany. I am ready to embark on a new journey.

Grandfather has always been grumpy, but he was becoming increasingly oppressive as my longing for independence grew by the day. It is difficult to say if it was his advancing years or my own growing maturity that was causing the trouble. At every turn, he blocked my desire to enter adult society, despite the fact that I will be seventeen in two weeks' time. He was especially obstructive in anything that had to do with Johann, as though he felt it his duty to protect me from my own heart's desire.

Its own foolish, foolish desire.

I still blush to recall the evening when I encountered him on the street and confessed my love to him . . . only to be rebuffed. He told me it was a childish fancy, although he is only eighteen to my sixteen. I have never felt so humiliated!

I loved him with my heart and soul. And he rejected them both — heart and soul. With just a few harsh words, he bled them from me, leaving a shell of a girl.

I can never face him again. Had he accepted my heart and soul, had he entwined his future with mine, I never would have left. But as soon as that part of me died — killed with the very weapon I'd handed to him — I knew I had to leave at once. And that, Diary, is why I left, under the cover of darkness, to meet Ingrid and Baron Frankenstein. It is so fortunate that this unexpected inheritance has given me a reason to leave Ingolstadt, otherwise my shame and hurt would have made my life there unbearable.

How I wish I could purge Johann from my heart, and more urgently from my mind, for he plays there endlessly, laughing in my face. I have run all this way to be free of my foolish love for a boy who never paid attention to me. Here in Gairsay I hope I can wipe the memory of him clean.

We have just entered Millburn Bay, and the rather small Gairsay Harbor has now come into view. I see no town, only a few wooden harbor buildings and one main dock.

I am too excited to write any longer and must tuck you, Dear Diary, away in my bag as I prepare to disembark. I'm anxiously awaiting a sight of Ingrid and Baron Frankenstein. . . .

CHAPTER THREE

June 7, 1815

The wind is so wild here! It blows and blows and blows. Everything is flying around, always! The sound of it has gotten into my head and almost stops me from thinking. I hope I get used to it, otherwise I don't know how I will survive living on this island. And I've only been here several hours.

It was nearly five in the late afternoon when a small two-sailed boat entered Millburn Bay, its sails filled. Uncle Ernest (I have come to refer to Baron Frankenstein as "uncle" as he has asked me to) and I were sitting on a bench at the end of the long dock. The tails of his coat beat against the bench like a flag rapping its pole in a hard breeze. For me, just keeping hold of my black, brimmed bonnet was a challenge.

Standing, I shaded my eyes from the still bright sun, since my hat was not wide enough to do the job. "She's here!" I cried.

"Good God! Your sister is a great beauty," Uncle Ernest noted as Giselle waved from the bow. Men, old and young alike, are often transfixed by their first view of Giselle's startling looks.

"And you are identical twins, you say?" he asked, looking at me critically.

It wasn't the first time someone had noted how different Giselle and I are in personal style. And it is never to my advantage. Where we both have the same abundant, nearly black curls, hers are piled high on her head with delicate coils at her forehead. I wear mine more simply, swept back in a braid, plaited from the upper quadrant of my skull, falling down my back.

We couldn't be more different in our manner of dress either. Giselle adores rich fabrics, stylish empire-waist dresses, and fashionable feather-trimmed bonnets, while a simple smock over a comfortable skirt and top are fine by me. (Whenever I can get by without a hat, I avoid one altogether.)

"Yes, we are exactly identical, biologically," I confirmed as Giselle approached. Having abandoned her luggage on the dock, she held her feathered bonnet in her hand, her dark hair uncharacteristically disheveled from the wind. "But we are entirely

different in personality and presentation. You'll have no difficulty telling us apart."

Uncle Ernest nodded. "You are the inquisitive one," he said.
Reaching over, he squeezed my shoulder consolingly, as if sympa-
thizing with my plight as the less attractive sister. "You are lovely
too, in your own way."

"It's fine," I assured him. "Giselle is wonderful. We are very close."

"Of course you are," Uncle Ernest replied.

How happy I was to see my twin! We embraced, both of us
delighted that the long months of separation were over at last.
When one is a twin, it is more than merely having a sibling. Other
sisters might be affectionate but they can never know the feeling of
being one with another human that twins enjoy.

Giselle pulled back from my arms to scrutinize me. "Italy has
agreed with you," she pronounced. "All that wonderful Italian
cooking has filled out your figure beautifully!"

This made me terribly self-conscious. "The food was divine,
but I ate too much of it!" I confessed.

"Nonsense! You were too bony before, but now you can fit into
some of the gorgeous dresses I bought while I waited for my connecting train in Paris. They're crammed into my luggage and no
doubt need a good pressing, but how could I resist? It was Paris,
after all!"

"Of course! You could not be expected to resist."

"Did you see the art in Italy?" Giselle wanted to know.

"Not very much of it, sadly. Count Volta kept me much too busy for trips to museums."

"What a loss," Giselle mourned. "If I had gone to Italy, it would have been the first thing I did. To have been in the land of Michelangelo and da Vinci . . . Caravaggio . . . and not seen —"

Baron Frankenstein coughed to get our attention.

"This is our uncle, Ernest Frankenstein," I said, embarrassed that I had forgotten he was there.

Uncle Ernest bowed formally. "At your service."

Giselle extended her hand and Uncle Ernest kissed it gallantly. "How wonderful to meet you!" Giselle said. "Do you resemble our father?"

"There is some resemblance, yes," Uncle Ernest admitted.

I know this will sound strange, but I am still getting used to the idea of having a father. There are so many questions I have!

For Giselle, however, the questions moved quickly to the next topic. "How soon can we arrive at the castle?" she asked.

"It is not a long way," Uncle Ernest assured her.

"No coach?" Giselle inquired, her dark arched brows lifting quizzically. She searched the area for a carriage we might hire.

Uncle Ernest indicated a roughly dressed farmer several yards farther off who wielded a pitchfork as he tossed hay onto the back of his horse-drawn cart. "We might engage that fellow for a ride, if you would prefer," Uncle Ernest offered.

Giselle wrinkled her delicate nose in distaste. "Where would we sit?"

"In the back," Uncle Ernest replied.

"Too itchy," Giselle decided, shaking her head.

"Perhaps he can bring our luggage to the castle." Uncle Ernest left us and approached the farmer.

While he was off negotiating, I hugged Giselle once more. "Have you seen the castle yet?" she asked eagerly.

"No. We only arrived a half hour before you did. We stayed here at the harbor to await you. How was your journey?"

Before she could answer, Giselle was seized with a fit of violent coughing. She buckled forward, turning red. I became worried by the intensity of the attack.

"Are you ill?" I asked.

"I am exhausted and can't get rid of this cough," she confided when she finally stopped.

"Poor dear," I said. "You can rest now. You have a whole castle in which to recover!"

This seemed to lift her spirits somewhat. "I can't wait to see it," she said.

As she spoke, I glanced to Uncle Ernest and saw that the farmer was shaking his head. For his part, Uncle Ernest had taken out his wallet and was proffering more and more coins.

"The man doesn't want to take us," I observed.

Giselle sighed unhappily. "I packed only what I needed, but I can't drag my bags all the way up there."

When Uncle Ernest returned we questioned him about what had happened. "Did he refuse to take our bags?" I asked.

"He was unwilling at first, but I finally offered him more money than he could stand to refuse."

"Why was he unwilling?" Giselle pressed.

"I'm sure that it's no matter for concern," Uncle Ernest assured us. "The man tells me that the people of this island think the castle is a fearful place. At least that's what I think he said. Though I spent many summers on this island when I was young, I have not been here for some time, and the heavy dialect spoken by the people confuses me. He might have said it was a sinful place. I do not recall the locals having such a fear when I was a boy. Now they seem to think some evil surrounds the castle."

Giselle and I exchanged a quick, worried glance. "Why would they think that?" I asked.

There was an anxious flicker in Uncle Ernest's gray eyes that belied the confidence of his words. "It hasn't been inhabited in a long time, and these are superstitious people."

"How long has it been empty?" Giselle inquired.

"Your father was the last of the Frankenstein family to stay there, and then only briefly. It was back in seventeen ninety-eight, I believe. The farmer says they have seen lights on in the place, especially during the long dark days of winter, when they experience only six hours of sunlight here. But no one ever comes or goes from the castle."

"Six hours of sunlight!" I couldn't believe my ears.

"We're not that far from Scandinavia and the Arctic Circle," Uncle Ernest explained. "It's spring, so now the hours of daylight will grow long. By the summer solstice, the sun will shine for up to eighteen hours."

"What's that like?" I asked.

"Those were happy times. Victor and I spent our summers here, running free. The long days only added to our fun."

I placed a kindly hand on his arm. "Do you miss him?"

"Victor was never dull," Uncle Ernest replied. I thought his answer evasive but it satisfied Giselle, who smiled and nodded. "Come!" Uncle Ernest said decisively. "This island is small. Our walk will be brief."

We began to hike up a winding country road. I enjoyed the constant crash of surf interlaced with the squawk of seabirds. Low rock walls lined our path on either side. Beyond them were rolling fields upon which sheep and goats grazed contentedly. There were breeze-rippled carpets of verdant green with only occasional patches of brown. Heather was scattered everywhere, as though some giant being had tossed it carelessly across the landscape.

A warm, humid breeze made my braid dance behind me and ruffled what was left of Giselle's elegant hairstyle. Uncle Ernest took off his hat to keep it from blowing away.

The path grew narrower as we crested the hill. Finally we pushed our way through a patch of blueberry bushes that obstructed our view. Without meaning to, I gasped. Giselle gripped my hand, wide-eyed.

Castle Frankenstein towered before us. Backed by the brilliant blue of the sky, the minerals of its stone walls sparkled in the sunlight. Windows were etched so deeply into the rock that they seemed to me like small caves. Two wide towers looked out onto the tempestuous waters leading out to the Atlantic Ocean.

Uncle Ernest strode toward the massive castle. "Come, girls! Let's see how this old giant has stood the test of time!"

Still holding my hand, Giselle pulled me forward. Suddenly frightened, I resisted her.

"What's the matter, silly?" she asked, smiling.

Despite the crisp blue day, the castle was dark and foreboding. Something within me warned not to go near it.

Giselle looked over her shoulder to see Uncle Ernest hurrying away from us. "Don't be nervous," she said, turning back toward me. "It will be fine. Fine!"

"You're not frightened?" I asked.

Bending forward with her arm to her face, Giselle began to cough once more. The deep hacking worried me tremendously. Giselle had always been delicate, and it did not surprise me that the long journey had depleted her health. I wondered how she would fare in this damp, windy place.

When Giselle's fit had subsided, she came beside me, flushed from coughing. "Of course I'm frightened," she said seriously. "But what choice is there? It's too late to turn back now. Our only way is forward."

For a moment, our eyes locked in silent communication. I knew that she was right. Grandfather had not wanted either of us to come to Gairsay, but we had defied him and been disowned for our disrespect. Now the inheritance from our father was our only means of support.

"Let's get you inside out of this wind," I said, rubbing between her shoulder blades. Nodding, she pulled in a deep breath in which I detected a shiver. And so we hurried forward, eager to discover what Castle Frankenstein would hold for us, yet afraid of what we might find.

CHAPTER FOUR

FROM THE DIARY OF

GISELLE VON DER WIEN

June 7, 1815

Castle Frankenstein has set my imagination ablaze with ideas of both its past and its future. It is broken-down, disheveled, filled with insects and cobwebs; damp, leaky, drafty — and yet when I imagine how I can convert the rooms to my liking it fills me with excitement. The place is a blank slate, a tabula rasa, on which I can imprint my own vision. As we walked through the high-ceilinged open spaces of the castle, Baron Frankenstein bemoaned the decline of its condition, shaking his head woefully and muttering what a shame it was that the place had been allowed to fall into such disrepair.

At one point I stopped to run my fingers along the thick, wavy, and bubbled stained glass of the windows. I was distracted, imagining how I could convert the rooms to my liking, and when I turned to ask Uncle Ernest a question, he and Ingrid were gone.

Searching for them, I came upon Baron Frankenstein standing alone in an empty room that looked out over the ocean. The poor man's eyes were filled with sadness. "I once sat here with my beloved mother, and she told me and Victor thrilling tales of giants and ogres in this countryside, a legacy from the Vikings who once raided and ruled here," he said when he saw I was observing him. "Victor loved the stories."

"Were you and my father close?" I asked politely.

"Victor was a wonderful brother," Baron Frankenstein stated passionately. "As a boy he was full of imagination, but eventually it overtook him. He imagined too much! He was insatiable for knowledge and it drove him mad. In the end I didn't know him at all — nor did I wish to know him. When he returned from the university, he wasn't the brother I knew, but rather an agitated, paranoid lunatic, always looking over his shoulder for an imagined enemy."

"We know next to nothing about our father, except that we have heard people call him a genius," I said. "Do you think that his genius drove him out of his mind?"

"Yes. But there was more to it than that. It was as though something had happened to make him shun family and friend alike."

The man was shaking, and the heartfelt passion of his words was alarming. I stepped back to create some distance from them, for the idea that we had a father who had gone mad was not pleasing to me. Ingrid would remind me that such traits can be handed down from parent to child.

Baron Frankenstein dashed the mist from his eyes and addressed me with more composure. "Will you be so kind as to find your sister and join me here? This seems as good a place as any to conduct the business of your inheritance. I see no reason to delay."

After nearly ten minutes of searching the vast castle, I came upon Ingrid in a small fifth-floor room where a narrow, glassless window revealed the vivid blue of the sky. She sat on the floor, engrossed in a large, thick, yellowed notebook. Looking up at me, her violet eyes shone with excitement. "These are our father's writings," she told me, "and they are amazing."

Settling on the floor beside her, I gazed down at the crumbling paper and saw the hurried, jagged scrawl indicative of an author in an agitated state. In contrast to the sloppily dashed annotations were biological illustrations rendered with impeccable precision; body parts of every sort were labeled and in some cases crossed out.

"Look at these drawings! Aren't they remarkable?" Ingrid gushed.

"They are truly impressive," I said, pulling the drawings closer.

"There are more notebooks," Ingrid said, pointing to a dusty stack of thick books across the room.

"Are they journals?" I asked.

"Yes, they seem to be both scientific *and* personal," Ingrid revealed.

With a clap of dust, she flipped to the front of the notebook, which was filled with scientific formulas. "I'm getting to a section where I'm having difficulty following what he's talking about," she admitted. "Since this is the first of the notebooks, it starts back in Geneva, before he even gets to university. I can follow some of what he says back then, as a boy of sixteen. He's very interested in the ancient science of alchemy, and I can comprehend some of what he's saying since I've read up on it a bit myself."

"Alchemy?" I asked, having never heard the word.

Ingrid sighed and sat back on her heels. "It's a very ancient science that attempts to transform simple metals into gold and silver."

"But our father was mad," I told Ingrid. "Baron Frankenstein told me so."

I thought this news would disturb Ingrid as it had disturbed me. But instead she asked thoughtfully, "Aren't all geniuses a bit mad?"

"I don't know," I admitted. "In my opinion, no amount of brilliance is worth it if you're also deranged. What possible good can come of a madman's work?"

Ingrid shook her head, and I could see from the fire in her eyes that she was not taking any of this lightly. "He was not mad when he was sixteen and wrote these things," she insisted, tapping the notebook.

"But isn't believing in alchemy like believing in magic?" I suggested.

"Count Volta doesn't think so," Ingrid said. "Although he never said so publicly, one day he told me that his work with metals and electricity made him more convinced than ever that the alchemists were onto something since they were involved in working with metals. He and his mentor, Luigi Galvani, created current by making positive and negative metals. Galvani proved that animal body parts could be brought to life by running current through them."

"But that's not making gold," I pointed out.

"Isn't that gold of a sort? Or greater, even, than gold?"

"Are you saying that reenergizing body parts is the same as creating gold?" I asked skeptically.

"Isn't it?" Ingrid answered.

This was too complex for me to consider, and it still struck me as a sort of lunacy, proof that what Baron Frankenstein had said about our father being mad was true.

Standing and extending my hand, I drew Ingrid up to her feet. "Baron Frankenstein has documents for us to sign before he can give us our inheritance, and we've kept him waiting too long already."

Ingrid's brows knit as she looked down at the notebook, almost as though she hated to leave it behind.

"You can return to it later," I assured her. I began to pull her along, but I felt a cough rise in me and had to drop her hand. I attempted to cover this action, but she knew me too well. I tried to grab her hand again, but she hesitated, much as she had before entering the castle.

"Giselle," she said, her voice full of concern, "are you sure we want to stay here? It's cold and drafty with only the barest of old furniture. I'm afraid your health will suffer. Maybe we should leave while the sea is still crossable. We will have money and can stay at an inn. Afterward, we can buy a more sensible home anywhere we want."

I walked her to the tall, narrow window and gazed out on the dark, swirling ocean. "It's incredible here, Ingrid," I said, thinking again of all the possibilities I could bring to it. "This is a gift that has fallen to us. We have to take it."

Ingrid nodded, and I could tell she was nearly convinced.

"You'll promise me that you won't let your health suffer?" she checked.

"I won't," I confirmed. "This fresh air will do me good."

"All right, then."

Another cough tickled my throat, but I fought it down because a coughing fit was the last thing I needed at the moment. I forced a smile and beckoned for Ingrid to follow me back down the stairs.

It was time to claim the Frankenstein fortune as our own.

CHAPTER FIVE

FROM THE JOURNAL OF

INGRID VON DER WIEN

June 7, 1815

Standing on the cliff's edge, I gazed out over the ocean, thinking about my new life. I could do this. I had to. It was the chance of a lifetime.

Gazing around, I noticed something that I'd missed earlier. There were no trees on the island. There was only ocean, low stone walls, and rolling fields. I had no idea where the hundred inhabitants could be living, since only two buildings were in sight of the castle.

Looking down into the ocean, it was easy to see another small, rugged island not very far out. There was a tumbled-down stone-and-thatch hut located on it. I couldn't imagine who might live in such a place and, indeed, it appeared abandoned.

The other visible building was to the right of the castle. It was a white, one-story cottage with a thatched roof. Smoke puffed from its single chimney though the day was warm.

Gazing back at the castle, I saw Giselle approaching. She came to my side and hooked her arm in mine. "We're rich," she said quietly.

"We're rich," I agreed.

"Now we have nothing to worry about." She's always known how and when to soothe me.

"Nothing to worry about," I echoed, and saying it made me feel it was so.

We returned to the castle to find Uncle Ernest asleep in one of the few chairs, snoring with an impressive resonance. On a nearby table he had thoughtfully laid out some of the cheese and bread I recalled him buying back in Aberdeen that morning. We devoured it, both of us discovering we were famished.

The food made us realize just how fatigued we were from the long, eventful day, but there was no obvious place to settle down. Furthermore, we needed to escape the roar of Uncle Ernest's snores.

In pursuit of sleep, Giselle and I climbed the stone stairs — perilously steep, winding, and slippery. On the second floor, we spied a room with a dusty purple velvet couch as its only piece of furniture. "You take it," I offered. With a nod, Giselle stripped down to her muslin chemise, unbuttoned her ankle boots, unpinned her bun so that her hair tumbled to her shoulders, and curled up, drawing her fringed Indian-print shawl over her as a blanket.

Continuing upward on my own, I found no other furnished room and so returned to the place where I'd discovered my father's books. The room was still awash with soft light, and I guessed it was around seven or so in the evening. It might have been later. I can already tell that the strange brightness of the overly long days here makes it difficult to gauge time exactly. Hopefully with practice I will get better at it.

Sitting with my back to the wall, I opened my father's notebook to the place where I had left off reading. By this point in his journal, Victor Frankenstein was a new student at the University of Ingolstadt and wrote of his first days there. He attended lectures where the subject was how lifeless flesh could be animated. Some said it was sacrilege to even think of this, as only God could bring life. Other scholars argued that if God had not meant for mankind to uncover this secret, it would be unknowable.

I am fascinated.

Here is the kind of high-level intellectual, scientific endeavor that is closed to me due to my gender. Yet I am living it through my father's words.

I will continue to read on, though I am getting very tired.

June 8

Several hours ago I was awakened, still lying on the floor with my father's notebook open on my lap. Darkness had finally filled the room, brightened only by a line of crystal moonlight shining through the narrow window.

I felt disoriented, unsure of where I was. My eyes flitted across the room, searching for signs of my old bedroom in Ingolstadt. And then I remembered.

I heard footsteps and the sound of a female voice murmuring. It came from out in the hallway and was getting nearer. Immediately I thought of what the Orkneyans had said about the castle — that someone was living in it, that they saw lights on at night.

Gooseflesh spread across my body as I slowly rose to standing. With trembling hands, I reached down to unbuckle my boot and slipped one foot out, and then took off the other as well. The low, chunky heel of the boot was the only weapon at my disposal.

The shuffling steps grew closer. I considered calling out for help but doubted my sleeping sister or uncle would hear me. I was two floors above them.

I could hear the approaching voice more clearly now. Its tone was snarling and fitful.

Lifting my boot high over my head, I braced, preparing to strike with the heel.

Suddenly a moon-rimmed figure appeared in the doorway.

"Giselle!" I cried.

Heart pounding, I slumped with relief and lowered my arm.

Giselle stood there dressed in her chemise, her shawl wrapped around her. Her lovely hair fell around her shoulders, glistening in the moonlight.

"You scared me," I scolded mildly, covering my pounding heart with my hand.

Giselle did not answer me. Nor did she move.

"I said you scared me," I repeated.

"Get away from me," Giselle muttered in a dark, threatening tone. It was her own voice, but the menacing quality was one I had never heard from her. "I'm warning you," she snarled.

Not only was her manner of speech unfamiliar to me, but so was her posture. She hunched like a cornered animal, undecided whether to flee or attack.

"It's me, Ingrid," I said, stepping forward and reaching toward her. "I didn't mean to scare you. I must have fallen asleep while reading the —"

"I TOLD YOU TO GET BACK!"

Giselle had never shouted with such ferocity in all our lives. I leapt away from her, frightened that she might strike me.

In the next moment, Giselle crumbled onto her knees. She began to make choking sounds and to gasp as though she couldn't get enough air. Deep, wailing sobs engulfed her and shook her delicate frame. It was heartbreaking in its awfulness.

Kneeling beside her, I attempted to console her by placing a tender hand on her back. She shook me off with a violent shudder.

I turned to see Uncle Ernest shuffling down the hall toward us, a flickering lantern in his hand.

Giselle's head jerked up as the light hit her. Her face was awash in terror. "No!" she screamed, jumping to her feet. She shielded her face from the light and turned away as though its low heat were scorching her. "No!"

"She's asleep," I told Uncle Ernest.

Putting down his lantern, he did what I've been told never to do: He grabbed hold of Giselle and shook her. Giselle's eyes widened with fear as though the very gates of Hell had opened in front of her and she was viewing its most inner spaces.

Giselle shuddered from head to foot before she fell into a dead faint. Uncle Ernest scooped her up and turned to carry her down the hall, her nightgown trailing to the stone floor. "Bring the lantern," he instructed, speaking to me from over his shoulder.

Uncle Ernest returned Giselle to the bedroom where she had settled down for the night. After I was satisfied that her breathing was steady and untroubled, I covered her once more with her coat and shawl. Then I joined Uncle Ernest out in the hall.

"Come downstairs with me for a while," Uncle Ernest requested. "There are things I must tell you about Castle Frankenstein."

CHAPTER SIX

FROM THE DIARY OF

GISELLE VON DER WIEN

June 7? June 8?

As I lay on my little couch in the dark, my eyes fluttered open and the blackness surrounding me was so impenetrable that at first I didn't know where I was. An icy chill enfolded me and I was quaking to the depths of my being. The dark terrifies me and always has, ever since I was small. The idea of creatures moving in the blackness, creatures I cannot see, is too horrible to bear.

Fighting down panic, I searched in the pocket of my coat and found the small tin of two-inch phosphorus-tipped sticks I'd purchased at the station when I'd changed trains in Paris. Extracting one stick and scratching it on the rough surface provided on the tin, I soon held a small flame against the dark. With my small halo of light, I discovered the barest nub of a candle in a corner on the floor and eagerly lit it.

The cause of my jangled nerves was not only my fear of the dark but also the horrific nightmare that was slowly coming to my conscious memory. I shudder now to recount it, but do so in the hope that telling the tale will keep the dreadful scenario from returning when next I visit sleep.

In my dream I was once more crossing the water with the disagreeable Captain Ramsay, who, in the dream, was much taller than in real life. His face became a horrible mask of hatred and he rose, abandoning his tiller, and began twisting my wrist, causing me to cry out with pain. While I struggled, the forceful wind beat furiously at the sails as the uncontrolled mast snapped around, about to hit us.

The next thing I knew, I was blessedly awake. I heard Ingrid's voice out in the hall in a hushed conversation with my uncle. Maybe the nightmare had caused me to cry out in my sleep and my cries had brought them to my door. The last words I heard my uncle utter as they retreated were *Castle Frankenstein*.

My feet feel scuffed and in this last flickering of my candle I have just noticed they are dirty. Oh, dear. Have I been walking in my sleep again? I pray not, for this cursed condition has plagued me for a lifetime.

With sleep will come renewed vigor. And so, Dear Diary, goodnight. Wish me well that I do not return to the terrible world of nightmares.

CHAPTER SEVEN

FROM THE JOURNAL OF

INGRID VON DER WIEN

June 8 (continued)

"What is it I should know about the castle?" I asked Uncle Ernest when we were down in the same first-floor room where we had established our inheritance earlier.

He lit a gas lamp and set it on the table. The wind outside was so fierce that it whistled through the openings in the stone walls and rattled the partially open windows. From time to time breezes threatened to extinguish the flickering lamp, but the small wick fought valiantly and managed to stay lit.

Uncle Ernest sat at the table and gestured for me to take the chair nearest to him. "This castle was built by the Viking Sweyn

Asleifsson in eleven fifty-eight," he began. "He used it as a place to rest when he wasn't plundering the coast of Wales with his Viking crew."

"Eleven fifty-eight," I echoed, impressed by its age. I had never dreamed the castle was that old. "Has it always been inhabited?"

"No, there have been long periods when it lay empty, left to molder and decay. When my parents took it over, it was nearly overrun with vermin of every sort. But my mother, Caroline Beaufort Frankenstein, restored it beautifully. She entertained glamorous figures in the arts and sciences. It became a destination for anyone traveling through Europe."

"I imagine that's what Giselle wants to do," I confided.

"Wonderful!" Uncle Ernest exclaimed. "Victor loved this place as a boy, which is why it was left to him while I was bequeathed other properties. It would have made him happy to know his daughters were restoring it."

"Giselle will be the one overseeing repairs and decoration," I told him. "I am not useful in such things."

"It doesn't matter which of you does it, just so long as it is accomplished. I would very much like to see the castle returned to its most glorious period. How merry and lively the place was then." His smiling visage slowly darkened with worry. "But is the girl up to it? It's quite the undertaking, and she already seems delicate."

I considered his concern before replying, for it was a valid one. "It might be just the thing for Giselle," I speculated. I didn't know if I was speaking the truth, or merely my hope for the truth.

"I'm afraid you girls will not find much in the way of suitable beaux here on the island," he said.

"If I need to seek a husband, it may be that I will find one among the interesting people with whom Giselle intends to fill the castle," I answered. In truth, though, I had more interesting things on my mind most of the time than snaring a husband. Marriage was Giselle's aim. In her recent letters, she had mentioned a particular man she'd had on her mind. Her silence on the matter since her arrival was enough for me to know it had not worked out.

"An excellent plan," Uncle Ernest concurred. "I have known you only a short while, Ingrid, but I can see that you are of a quick mind, equal to your father's. Not just any man will hold your attention, so it's best if you find a young fellow of mental accomplishment."

I smiled at him. This sounded like an agreeable thing to me. A man with whom I could speak about the subjects that truly fascinated me would be a welcome companion. "For now, I want to read all of my father's journals, which I have discovered in that top room where you found me," I told Uncle Ernest. "That will be project enough for the time being."

"My brother's journals?" Uncle Ernest asked, paling. "Niece, I would far sooner you destroyed them than read them."

"Why?"

"My brother, your father, was an emotionally intense young man with a fevered intellect, and I fear the contents of those notebooks can only bring more questions of the sort that changed him, drove him mad. He left for university a passionate and rebellious boy. He loved fun and had friends before he went, but he returned utterly changed, wanting nothing to do with his family or former companions. He completely abandoned everything he once loved."

"The way he abandoned Ingrid and me?" I mentioned.

"Yes, but you and your sister are not alone in this, dear girl. Upon his return from university, he was aloof with everyone."

"Could it be that he was devastated by the death of my mother?" I asked. It seemed a reasonable possibility. A young man in love whose wife had recently died giving birth to his daughters might easily be consumed by grief. It was a scenario I had played out many times in my head. It was the only thing that could make his absence in our lives excusable.

"It is certainly possible. But there were other things," Uncle Ernest said.

"What sorts of things?" I was struck by the ominous tone of his voice.

Uncle Ernest leaned in closer, and the flickering lamp threw wavering shadows across his serious, lined face. "There was a period of several years when Victor was no longer at university and we had no knowledge of his exact locations. What finally brought him home to Geneva was the tragic news that our youngest brother, William, a mere child, was found dead. Murdered. We had to send his dear friend Henry Clerval to search for him in order to summon him home."

"How terrible," I sympathized. "Who killed William?"

"Our household maid Justine hung for the crime, and for a while I believed that justice had been done."

"But you don't think so anymore?"

"Not long after the maid's trial, Henry Clerval joined Victor on a tour of Europe. My brother said he needed a change of scenery to rest his mind. After they had toured the continent and England together, Victor requested that they go their separate ways, and Henry agreed. Victor came here to the castle while Henry went on to Ireland. While in Ireland, Henry was murdered."

I gasped. "Who murdered him?"

"Victor was charged by the Irish court with his murder."

This was too much to bear. First, to find out my father was dead. Now, to find out he was a murderer.

"Is that why he escaped to the Arctic?" I asked, barely able to contain the tremor in my voice.

"No, that came later. He was acquitted of the crime, Ingrid. Your father was many things, but he was *not* a murderer. His alibi was that he was here, and people on the island confirmed it. But that was also when people became afraid of the place. Clearly my brother was going mad up here all alone. Who knows what horrific experiments he was undertaking?"

"Have you read his journals, the ones I found upstairs?"

Uncle Ernest shook his head. "I never knew of their existence until today. As you know, it's been a long time since I've set foot here. I will confess I felt a selfish desire to leave the past alone."

"Perhaps, as I read through them, they will throw a light on his activities during that period."

"Is that really a good idea? I worry," Uncle Ernest said, "about what impact reading the ravings of a madman will have on such a young and impressionable mind as yours, especially knowing that this unbalanced individual is your own father."

"Perhaps he was not as insane as you believe," I suggested. "Genius can seem like lunacy to those of us who are too dull-witted to comprehend what the elevated mind perceives."

Grunting with disapproval, Uncle Ernest shook his head. "There is danger in an idea like that, Ingrid," he warned. "That you would entertain such a thought enlarges my concerns about your inherited inclinations. A man such as me has not my brother's brilliance, but I have had a good job, a wife who loved me well, and children now grown to capable adults. It has been a calm and orderly life that I have found most satisfying."

What he described seemed to me a life of utter boredom. But I was not so rude as to say so.

"My brother, for all his genius, left behind him a trail of misery and murder," Uncle Ernest added.

"But he was acquitted of the murder," I reminded him.

Locking his hands together behind his head, Uncle Ernest leaned back in his chair and sighed. His pensive expression told me he was considering his next words.

"I did not say he was a murderer," Uncle Ernest began slowly, "but certainly death followed him. In a very short span of time our younger brother lay slain, his best friend was murdered, and his second wife was killed."

"His *second wife*?" I asked. Was there no end to my father's secrets?

"Yes," Uncle Ernest said. "Elizabeth. She was adopted and grew up in the house with us, but since she was not a blood relative, she and Victor were free to marry. They were engaged when he left for university, but gradually he stopped writing to her as he did all of us, even Henry, myself, and our father. I often wondered if the reason he never came back home was because he was avoiding her, and couldn't stand to tell her he'd fallen in love with another."

"My mother?"

"I imagine so. But after your mother died, some years passed and Elizabeth waited for Victor's return with unbelievable commitment, and was rewarded — or so she thought — when he reappeared. As far as she knew, they were still engaged to be married. You must understand — none of us knew about you and your sister's existence. That only came to light after his death, when his final wishes were revealed."

The possibilities suggested by this new information made my head spin. Did Victor refuse to acknowledge us because he didn't want to tell his new wife that he had two living daughters? Once he remarried, had he intended to come claim us and have this Elizabeth raise us as a stepmother?

Then I remembered what Uncle Ernest had said.

His second wife was killed.

"What happened to her?" I asked.

"Murdered," Uncle Ernest reported.

"But how? Who?"

"On her wedding night. Strangled in her bed by some mysterious intruder." Ernest leaned forward, elbows on the table. "I remember that awful night so clearly. Victor was anxious the whole day, but I ascribed it to the wedding-day nerves of a groom. Now, in hindsight, it seems to me he had some foreboding of the calamity to come. When we discovered Elizabeth dead in her bed, he shouted, 'The fiend! The monster!' as though he knew — and had been expecting — her assailant."

"Who could it have been?" My every muscle was tense in anticipation of the answer.

Uncle Ernest shook his head wearily. "In all the years I have had to ponder these things, I have concluded that my brother had a powerful enemy who dogged his every step and preyed on his loved ones."

"Who would be so vengeful?"

"I don't know, but Victor must have greatly wronged this person."

"Could that be why he went to the Arctic, to draw this enemy away from those he loved?" I asked, knowing full well that *those he loved* included my sister and me.

"Very possibly. There have been no more murders in the last ten years."

Three murders in such a short period of time. It was indeed suspicious. Who was this powerful enemy? Did he live still? If so, was his vengeance spent?

"There is one man who might be able to shed some light on this mystery," Uncle Ernest added as he rose from the table and lifted the lantern. "About ten years ago, a Captain Robert Walton contacted me by mail, saying he had seen Victor stranded on an ice floe in Arctic waters. Apparently Victor had confided things to him that he only wished to speak of face-to-face. He suggested that we should meet to talk further. I immediately traveled to his widowed sister's house in London, as he suggested, but upon my arrival the sister informed me that Captain Walton had just set sail for St. Petersburg in Russia to sign onto another Arctic expedition of exploration."

"You never heard from him again?"

"I tried to contact the sister some years later, but was told by her landlady that she had remarried and moved away. Not knowing how else to proceed, I let the trail grow cold."

"I could try to find her," I suggested. "I plan to make trips to mainland Scotland and England. I could search for her while I'm there."

"Be careful, Ingrid," Uncle Ernest counseled. "Some secrets are best left buried."

"I don't agree," I countered. "It is always better to know the truth."

"Spoken like a truly deep thinker," he said with a faint and somewhat sad smile. "But I am not convinced."

CHAPTER EIGHT

FROM THE DIARY OF

GISELLE VON DER WIEN,

HENCEFORTH TO BE KNOWN AS BARONESS FRANKENSTEIN

June 10, 1815

Frankenstein is my name, so why shouldn't I use it? Baron Frankenstein assures me it is an old and venerable name of which I have every reason to be proud. I am my father's legitimate heir and am now the lady of Castle Frankenstein. Like my uncle, my father, Victor, was also a baron and this makes me, legitimately, Baroness Frankenstein, a title that I rather like and fully intend to embrace, especially as I will very soon be seventeen and ready to take my role in the adult world with money, property, and a title.

You're just a child, Johann said. And he might as well have added, *And you're a nobody, with nothing.*

How wrong I shall prove him.

I have decided to begin my renovation on the open and cavernous first floor, undertaking to begin with the most challenging and public space first. The ceilings of the entire ground level are at least twenty feet high, and to the left of the front entranceway is an immense room that would lend itself most excellently to grand dinners and balls.

It was while I was standing in the middle of the gigantic space, contemplating where to begin my renovation, that Ingrid and Baron Frankenstein came in. With them was a tall woman covered in a gray woolen cape. She had a chiseled angular face and her bright carrot-colored hair was caught in a severe bun.

Baron Frankenstein introduced us. "Giselle, meet Agnes Flett, who has agreed to be our housekeeper."

"We have just now hired her," Ingrid added.

"Welcome, Mrs. Flett," I said cordially. "I suppose the first order of things is to get you set up in a room."

I believe she said, "I suppose so," though it sounded more like "Ay sipasesi." Understanding the people on these islands is going to be a great challenge even more difficult than comprehending the Scots of the mainland, especially in the northern highlands where I found it all but impossible. Although I did well in language studies in Germany and am considered fluent in English, I never anticipated having to understand such a heavy dialect as this.

"We *all* must get set up with proper accommodations," Ingrid said. "I propose a trip to Edinburgh to purchase some furniture."

"Yes, the sooner the better," I agreed, already looking forward to the journey. I knew we'd have to settle in first and see what furniture could be salvaged from the castle as it stood. But eventually, we'd bring some newness to this very old place.

June 13, 1815

Mrs. Flett has turned out to be a wonder of industry, and set to work on the rooms almost immediately using what furniture we could scrape together. For the last few days, Ingrid and I worked with her until we were fairly exhausted from knocking down cobwebs and scrubbing floors. I fear we were more in the way than helpful, and today, after four hours, the indefatigable Mrs. Flett finally shooed us off to be out of her way. "Girls," she said before we left, "what do you say about letting me hire some of my kinsmen who live on the island to move things along?"

Ingrid and I looked to each other and then down at our work-weary hands. "That sounds like a wonderful idea, Mrs. Flett," I agreed, hoping I had understood her correctly. We certainly had the money for it now, so it seemed only sensible. "Hire whomever you'd like."

Glad to be set free, we walked out onto the property in front of the castle. Arm in arm, we strolled almost to the edge of the cliff overlooking the ocean, each holding a novel we were reading. I was in the midst of the gloriously amusing *Pride and Prejudice* by Jane Austen, but I couldn't see what book Ingrid had with her.

"It's called *The Devil's Elixirs*," she revealed when I questioned her about it. "It's a new publication by a man calling himself E. T. A. Hoffmann."

"It sounds frightening," I remarked.

"It is," Ingrid admitted. "Very frightening. And scandalous too! I'm sure Grandfather would never allow me to read it, but here we are on our own, and who's to stop me? It's the story of a monk who drinks the devil's special brew and then takes on the personality of his lunatic double, who is a prince. He winds up murdering his stepmother, and all manner of awful things happen."

I shivered, holding on to my bonnet to keep it from blowing off into the wind. "Why would you want to read such a thing?"

"Why not?" Ingrid countered. "It's exciting."

Laughing, I opened my novel, searching for the spot where I'd left off reading. "One would scarcely believe we were twins, we are so different," I commented.

With a shrug, Ingrid settled on the grass beside me and also opened her novel. I read for nearly fifteen minutes before looking up to discover that Ingrid had put her book aside and was instead gazing over at a white, one-story cottage about a half mile to our right.

"Bored with my company already?" I asked, teasing. "Looking for new friends?"

Ingrid smiled sheepishly, embarrassed at my observation. "Of course not — you know better than that," she chided. "I'm only wondering who lives over there."

"Just one of the simple folk of the island," I remarked with disinterest. "Hardly worth your time."

Ingrid raised her eyebrows and looked askance at me. "Isn't that rather snobbish of you?"

"Oh, please, Ingrid, don't be so false. Do you really want to strike up a friendship with some farmers with no education or culture? How much will you really have in common with them? If you open that door, you'll be ducking them at every turn before you know it." It may not have sounded warmhearted, but at least it was honest.

"We could be neighborly," Ingrid insisted.

The absurdity of that made me laugh. I imagined how that scene might unravel. "'Oh, hello, I'm Ingrid from the monstrously huge castle next door. What a cozy little hovel you have,'" I said, playing Ingrid's part.

"I wouldn't call that a hovel," Ingrid insisted as she stood, brushing grass from her skirt. She stepped toward the edge of the cliff and pointed down. "That hut on the small island down there — *that's* a hovel. The place to our right is a cottage. And you're right. It *does* look cozy."

"Have it your way," I conceded, not thinking the subject worth arguing about.

"I'm going over there to introduce myself," Ingrid stated firmly. "We have been here nearly a week, and I think it's rude of us not to say hello."

"Isn't it customary for the neighbors to come over to welcome *us*?" I countered. "Isn't it they who have been rude?"

"Aren't you always saying that we are nobles now? We should act like nobles."

"Oh, *really*, Ingrid!" I cried, exasperated by her stubbornness. "You couldn't care less about royalty, and are just using my interest in our new royal station to get your own way. They're probably not even there. Most likely they're out shearing the sheep or milking the goats or some such thing."

"There's smoke coming from the chimney."

"It's just your endless curiosity, you know."

"So what if it is?" Ingrid challenged. "There's nothing wrong with being curious about things."

"It's going to get you into trouble someday," I cautioned.

"It won't," Ingrid maintained as she straightened her bonnet, preparing to depart.

"It will." I watched Ingrid's determined stride as she walked away from me. "Ingrid, come back!" I shouted, but the wind snapped up my words and blew them out to sea.

CHAPTER NINE

FROM THE JOURNAL OF
INGRID VDW FRANKENSTEIN

June 13, 1815

(Giselle has convinced me to adopt the name but I am most definitely *not* going to call myself Baroness F. I would feel ridiculous.)

Today I met the most remarkable person.

Normally I might have felt shy about simply showing up at a stranger's door and introducing myself. But I had a few words with Giselle in which she admonished me not to bother meeting our only neighbor. This brought out the stubborn streak in my character as only my sister can, and I was determined to go.

Admittedly, a certain nervousness returned as I neared the

cottage. The place was surrounded by a waist-high wall made from stones and gave the impression of being extremely neat and well-tended. The white smoke puffing from the chimney told me that someone was home. Passing through the opening in the wall, I stepped up to the thick wooden door and knocked, fully expecting the woman of the house to answer.

After waiting for some minutes with no response, I walked around to the side. An all-white mare roamed freely, grazing. It whinnied when I appeared and then returned to its grassy meal. It wasn't fenced in, so I assumed the owner had no fear of it wandering off.

I tried to see in the windows, but the curtains were drawn, so I went back to rap on the door once more. This time I thought I detected the sound of someone shuffling about inside, which prompted me to bang on the door with more force.

Still, no one came.

I was on the verge of leaving when I saw movement at the window nearest the door. From behind the curtain, someone was sneaking a peek at the front door. Encouraged, I pushed stray wisps of hair back in my bonnet and waited. Soon the door pulled slowly inward.

"Hello?" I called after a moment of further waiting. When no one replied, I stood closer to the opening and called again, leaning into the warm, darkened room.

A large stone fireplace glowed in the center of the main room where I stood. Heavy timbers connected uneven walls with a wide planked wooden floor. On two walls, floor-to-ceiling shelves housed many books. This private library did not seem in keeping with such a rough-hewn cottage.

"Can I help you?"

I couldn't tell where the rich, low male voice had come from. The speaker was male and British. A certain strength in the resonant tone told me that he was not old.

"Over here." In a shadowed corner I finally saw the man who had spoken. Though I couldn't gauge his height while seated, he had broad shoulders and a head of luxuriant, nearly black curls that fell around his ears and neck. The fire sparked and lit half his face. Piercing amber eyes studied me. They were set beneath straight dark brows. His lips were full and his jaw square.

Summoning my nerve, I stepped more fully into the room, though I took the precaution of leaving the door slightly ajar. "I'm sorry to bother you," I began, and was dismayed to hear an uneasy scratchiness in my voice. "I am Ingrid Von . . . a . . . well, Ingrid will do —"

"Not sure of your own last name?" he interrupted.

An embarrassed smile formed on my lips. "No. I assure you I know my own name. It's . . . a long story."

"What isn't?" he remarked with an air of bitter irony.

"Ah, yes. I know what you mean," I replied, feeling idiotic, since I had no idea what he meant.

"What brings you here, Ingrid?" he asked. His voice was neutral.

"Nothing, really, except my sister and I just moved into the castle next door and —"

"'The castle next door'?" he echoed mockingly.

"Yes."

"The ancient, sprawling edifice of stone?"

"Yes."

"Oh, *that* castle. Now that you mention it, I think I've noticed it."

I was sure my cheeks were burning red, which only added to my mortification. Hopefully they were masked by the jumping shadows. "We have just now inherited it," I explained.

"Then your last name must be Frankenstein."

"Yes." Though it was still too soon for me to think of it as my own name yet

"No wonder you stammered over it."

"What do you mean by that?" I asked. Maybe he could tell me something about my father. Perhaps he would reveal more about why the local people were frightened of the castle.

"Nothing. I meant nothing at all."

With hands on hips, I eyed him with unabashed skepticism. "Tell me, please," I requested.

"It was nothing but boorishness on my part. I am unaccustomed to having pretty young women visit me in the middle of the day. I have been reclusive for so long I've quite lost all sense of civility."

"So I see," I allowed reluctantly, for I still did not believe there was *nothing* behind his comment. Why would someone say such a thing if he did not have a reason?

An awkward moment stretched between us. "Well, I am Ingrid Frankenstein, and I simply came over to introduce myself," I said to break the silence. I extended my hand to shake his. (I know this is not ordinarily the custom, but there was something straightforward about him that made it seem the right thing to do.) When he didn't rise to shake my hand, I realized he was fumbling with an ebony cane by the side of his chair. "Please don't get up," I urged, realizing that he was not having an easy time of it.

He grumbled angrily under his breath and continued his struggle. By gripping the chair with one hand and balancing on his cane with the other, he slowly came to stand. His rise went on longer than I'd have anticipated. By the time he was fully upright, he towered over me, possibly the tallest man I'd ever seen. He leaned so heavily on the cane that I realized he would have been taller still if he were not stooped by his disability.

"I am Walter Hammersmith," he said, leaning the cane against the table and taking my hand to shake. He used his left hand and I saw that his right arm hung limply at his side. But his left hand was strong and so massive that mine disappeared into his firm grip. I imagined this was what it might be like to shake hands with a bear. "To be more precise," he added, "I am Lieutenant Walter Hammersmith of the Royal British Army, retired."

Gazing up into those burning eyes, I saw that he was somewhere in his early twenties, possibly a little younger. "Aren't you young to be —"

"Retired?" he anticipated my question.

"A lieutenant," I said.

Walter looked back at his chair. "You'll forgive me if I sit. Standing tires me."

"Let me help you," I offered, taking his elbow. He fairly collapsed into the chair.

When he was seated, he bade me take my place in another nearby chair. "I am young to have been a lieutenant and I am young to be in this wretched condition you find me in, as well. We can thank Napoleon Bonaparte for both."

"Why Napoleon?"

"I owe both my rank and ill health to Napoleon, since one is often promoted more quickly in wartime and one also ages more rapidly in wartime due to stress, illness, and injury. If one is lucky enough to age at all, of course."

I have lived a sheltered life, but I have not been so protected that I did not know that Napoleon's French troops had been wreaking havoc across Europe, Russia, and even Egypt. "You fought the French troops?" I assumed.

"The Danes and Norwegians," Walter corrected me. "They were fighting against England as conquered nations under French control. I was in Lyngør, not very far from here. Three years ago, I was promoted and assigned to a gunboat."

"And that's where you were injured," I conjectured.

"It's a long story," he said dismissively.

This made me smile. "What isn't?" I said.

Recognizing he'd been caught, his face lit up, and for the first time I thought him quite handsome.

"There's no place I have to be and I'd love to hear your long story if you feel like telling it," I said sincerely.

"It's not a happy story," he warned.

"That's all right."

"Well, to be fair, my sorry condition isn't entirely due to Napoleon — or the Norwegians or the Danes, for that matter. I might have been able to get out of the way of their cannon fire had I not already been slowed down by an illness that has been slowly progressing since my late teens. I hid it from everyone, but in the end it caused me injury."

"How terrible! What illness is that?"

"The doctors don't understand much about it. They say it's a disease of the nervous system."

"Is there no cure?" I asked.

"No. There is not," Walter said. "Though I once consulted a doctor who believed electric current might be helpful in —"

"He was a student of Galvani?" I interrupted excitedly.

"You know of Galvani's experiment?" Walter was clearly surprised by this.

"I studied with Count Volta, a student of Galvani. Did you pursue the electric treatment?"

"I did not," he answered. "It seemed too dangerous. I have seen a man struck by lightning while standing atop a ship's upper mast during a storm. He quaked and shuddered, caught in the lines of the sails, jolted by the impact. I couldn't see why a man would willingly subject himself to such a shock."

"Even if it might cure you?"

"At the time, I didn't realize how far this illness would progress. The doctor who was willing to do this has since died."

"If he was alive, you might reconsider?"

"Perhaps."

Another awkward silence fell between us. My eyes had adjusted to the dimness and I took stock of the place. In the plain kitchen area I noticed shelves stocked with food. "Are you able to get on here by yourself with no help?" I dared to ask.

"A woman who lives on the island comes to look in on me."

"You pay her?"

"Yes."

Someone rapped on the front door and we both looked to it. Standing, I parted the drawn curtains and saw Giselle outside. "My sister," I reported. "She's probably worried about me. I'd better go."

"As you wish." A formal stiffness returned to Walter's tone.

"May I visit you again?" I asked, surprised by my own boldness.

"As you wish."

"You won't mind?" I questioned, suddenly insecure.

"No. I would welcome the company."

"Very well, then. I will come see you again."

"Should I meet your sister?" Walter asked.

"No. I've taken enough of your time," I said, heading for the door. "My sister wouldn't come with me, so she doesn't deserve the pleasure."

He laughed scornfully. "Quite a doubtful pleasure."

"I will see you soon," I promised quickly. For some reason, I was anxious to get out before Giselle came in.

When I was once again out in the bright, windy world, Giselle placed her hand on my arm. "I was getting concerned about you. Who lives there?"

"Just a grumpy, very old man," I lied.

I don't want to share Walter with her. I had discovered sad, sick Lieutenant Walter Hammersmith, and I wanted to keep him for myself.

CHAPTER TEN

FROM THE DIARY OF

BARONESS GISELLE FRANKENSTEIN

June 17, 1815

The days grow ever longer and warmer in this strange windy climate. It serves to make the place less forbidding. The fatigue and congestion I was feeling are slowly abating as I recover from my exhausting journey with long, dream-filled bouts of sleep. The constant crash of waves and calls of seabirds create a lullaby that I find deeply soothing, conducive to healing slumber.

Ingrid and I turned seventeen two days ago, and though there was no real way to celebrate, Baron Frankenstein bade Mrs. Flett to make a special dinner and a sumptuous cake. He gifted each of us with a jeweled broach from the estate of our grandmother Caroline Beaufort Frankenstein. Mine is in the form of an exotic bird with long, draping, emerald-laden feathers; for Ingrid, he selected a rose pin with rubies.

With my renewed energy, the undertaking of the castle's restoration seems less daunting. I am convinced that it has a life that belongs to it alone, as though it were a living creature. With the aid of the very capable Mrs. Flett, it is gradually showing signs of returning to its former self, much like a recovering patient who day by day regains the glow of his former health.

Mrs. Flett has lived on Gairsay from the dawn of time and seems to be related to every soul on the island, nearly all of whom share the bright orange locks they claim to have inherited from their forbearers, the Vikings. This I have no difficulty believing, as they — the men in particular — are as strong, rough, and in some cases as savage as those Nordic plunderers of old.

Thankfully, the good Mrs. Flett knows how to harness all the raw energy of her unruly relatives into a most impressive group of workers, and has employed nearly all of the young men in the restoration of the castle. Whatever misgivings they may have had about the place have been overcome by the appeal of the steady pay that will last at least until the castle is as I desire it to be, which I estimate to be months away. Crude and boisterous as these young men are, I have to admit that their shouts and laughter have enlivened the place considerably and dispel a great deal of the ominous feel of the castle, at least during the day.

There is one young man in particular who holds me in a most bold, direct gaze every time I pass by. His insolence should anger me, yet I find it difficult not to make eye contact with him. He is strikingly handsome in a rough sort of way, with orange hair to his shoulders and a well-muscled torso that he displays when his arms lift. The other day I controlled myself until I thought I was well past him, then gave into the urge to sneak a glance. He was still looking at me, and our eyes locked for a flash before I averted mine. Even though I was turned away, I could feel him grinning with triumph.

As I turned to leave, I ran right into Mrs. Flett and jumped back in surprise. "Don't let Riff bother you," I think she said, although it sounded more like "Dunna le Riff ba ye." The best I could make out of the rest of her words amounted to the fact that Riff chases all the girls on the island and catches most of them. Honestly, Diary, I can see why. He has a sort of strange magnetism, though he certainly is not someone I would ever be interested in.

Riff kept watching while I spoke to Mrs. Flett. Noticing, she shooed him off with a wave of her hand until, with an obnoxious smirk, he finally turned away. From now on I shall go out of my way to avoid him whenever he is near.

It makes me sad that Ingrid does not partake in the excitement of the renovation. Now that Baron Frankenstein has departed for Scotland to visit with an associate in Edinburgh, Ingrid is my only company, and she has spent all of this past week in that tower room, poring over the volumes of our father's work that she discovered on the first day we were here. Occasionally I can persuade her to take a walk with me in the front grounds overlooking the ocean, but when we do venture out, she is so hopelessly lost in thought that she's not much of a companion.

"Don't become like our father," I joke.

She doesn't find much humor in this statement, and her sour reaction makes it less of a joke than it had been when I made it.

Often I see that she's looking over at the little cottage to the right of the castle, as though she expects to see smoke signals forming in the puffs of white smoke that lift relentlessly from the chimney stack.

"What do you find so intriguing about the old man who lives there?" I asked yesterday, and Ingrid seemed not to know what I was referring to.

"Old man?" she asked me blankly as we stood at the edge of the cliff overlooking the ocean, the wind whipping our skirts.

"You told me an unhappy old man lives there," I reminded her, exasperated.

"Oh, yes!" Ingrid recalled. "Well, perhaps he's not as old as I made him out to be."

"How old is he?" I demanded.

"Hard to tell exactly," she replied. "Not as old as I thought at first. In fact, he's not that much older than we are."

"Not much older than we are? Then he's not old at all! How could you have made such an error?"

"It was dark and he's ill. I told you that," Ingrid snapped.

I was quite taken aback by her peevishness; it's not like Ingrid to be so easily vexed, and her reaction bewildered me. "What's wrong with him?" I asked.

She told me that a nerve disease had wreaked devastating effects on his body and that he'd been wounded by cannon fire from Napoleon's war. As she explained, there was such tender sympathy in her eyes as I have never seen there before.

"Will you go see him again?" I inquired.

"I think I will," she said. "He strikes me as someone deeply in need of a friend."

"You're sure he's quite sane?" I checked. "From what you describe, he seems rather odd. Is there any threat of danger in being there with him alone?"

"He's safe enough, and there's no violence in him. But he is tormented by a profound unhappiness."

"He's ill," I pointed out.

"Even so, it's not proper for you to be there alone with him so much," I pointed out.

"He's always a gentleman!" Ingrid cried, vexed by my inference. "And I don't care a thing for what others might think."

"This is a small island, Ingrid. People will talk."

"Let them! We've done nothing wrong!"

"He is a dark and brooding man," I reminded her. "That's what you have told me. He may be more unpredictable than you think. Perhaps his illness is driving him mad."

"He's not mad, I tell you! Instinct tells me that there is some very sad secret in his past. If only I knew what it was."

"What could you do, even if you knew?"

"I would help him to rise above it."

"Some secrets are best left unrevealed," I commented.

We stood in silence for a few moments more, each looking out over the ocean, lost in thought. It occurred to me that Ingrid had not answered my original question, so I asked it once more. "What do you find so intriguing about Walter Hammersmith?"

"What do you find so intriguing about Castle Frankenstein?" she countered.

"I envision it as it must have once been. I imagine its former grandeur and long to return it to the glory it once possessed," I answered.

Ingrid gazed out over the ocean a few moments before answering.

"Yes. That's how I feel about Walter Hammersmith, exactly the same way."

"I can restore the castle, but you can never bring Walter Hammersmith back."

"I can," she insisted.

"How?" I challenged.

"With love."

"Love?"

"And science," she added.

"Ingrid, you worry me."

She smiled grimly. "I worry myself."

"You mentioned love. Do you love him?"

"As one human loves and feels compassion for another," she replied, but I didn't believe her.

She was clearly enamored of this sick and morose individual who could never be a suitable husband to her. "You are getting involved too deeply with this man. Stop now: Don't go there anymore," I beseeched her.

Ingrid sighed, and it occurred to me that she had been sighing quite a lot lately. "I have to go," she insisted before turning back to the castle. "Please don't try to stop me," she added as she walked off.

I am so worried about her reputation as well as her emotional well-being. I know not what she has in her mind but no good can come of it, I'm afraid. If only this Walter Hammersmith would simply disappear, my mind would rest so much easier.

June 17 (continued)

Oh, Diary! The thing I both dreaded and dreamed of has happened, and I don't know what to do!

The mail here comes about once a week, brought over from the mainland of Scotland by boat. In the near fortnight since we arrived, the boat hadn't brought a single piece of correspondence, even though I have written to several of my friends from Ingolstadt.

But this afternoon, I received a letter from Johann.

It is the first letter he's ever written to me, so I did not recognize the hand at first. But once I opened the envelope, I knew.

My breath was quite knocked out of me.

Before I could read a single word, I was dizzy with questions: How had he found me? Why had he written?

In order to read in private, I hurried out to the cliff overlooking the ocean and, with trembling hands and racing pulse, I read it. Dear Diary, it is no exaggeration to say that his words have shaken and stunned me, as they are wholly unexpected.

I have used sealing wax to attach the letter here:

Dearest Giselle,

I hope you are well and that your grand adventure is everything you dreamed. Please don't mind me writing to you. I received your new address from your friend Margaret. (She promises to correspond soon.)

I was happy to find out where to write to you since I feel badly about how things were left between us. It has occurred to me that you must be suffering from wounded feelings since I thought it necessary to be harsh with you the last time we spoke. Previously I may have put a distance between us, but did so only because I was involved in an intimate correspondence with a girl in Geneva. I broke off that relationship because of my feelings for you, but unfortunately this happened right at the time when you felt compelled to leave.

I had no idea that you had inherited a castle until I learned it from Margaret. I thought you had run off because of my hard words to you and have suffered the tortures of the damned, plagued as I am with guilt for hurting such a delicate soul as yours. I hope you can see now that it was to protect your feelings and your honor that I deemed it the right thing to do to push you away.

As it turns out, my father and I will be traveling to Scotland within the month to consult with a client in the city of Edinburgh. I wonder if I might be so bold as to suggest that we might meet while I am there. My father or your newfound uncle could chaperone. Please think upon this and let me know. I will write you with the exact dates once I know your feelings. I hope

perhaps that this meeting will rekindle the fond emotions that once you
honored me by bestowing. I am sincerely

Yours,

Johann

With mixed emotions, I folded the letter and tucked it into the pocket of my dress. Of course I feel elation: This is my fondest dream come true. But I am also confused by this change of heart. The story about the girl in Geneva might be true, I suppose, though my friends who are closer to Johann than I was have never alluded to it. On the contrary, they assured me there was no specific rival other than the many girls who, like me, admired him from afar.

Perhaps it is only that distance has made him appreciate me more or that his letter is, in fact, true, and he is now free and taking the opportunity to act on what he had also felt deep down. I find myself hoping this is so, and will trust that emotion to be my guide.

I will write him immediately to say I will be Edinburgh with my uncle, and then write to Baron Frankenstein, entreating him to let Ingrid and me join him there.

Johann spurned me as a young girl, and now I see he may have been right. But I am different now. If he saw me as I am here, he would find no trace of youth. I have become his equal.

Dear Diary, I am filled with happiness!

CHAPTER ELEVEN

FROM THE JOURNAL OF

INGRID VDW FRANKENSTEIN

June 18, 1815

I read and read without ever being bored for as long as there is daylight. (And every day the light lasts longer and longer. This morning it was light by four in the morning and stayed so until eleven at night. The night was more like dusk, lacking any true blackness.)

Hunger drove me to set the journals aside and wander down the winding stairs to seek food. I wasn't halfway down when the din of boisterous workmen hammering, sawing, shouting, and occasionally laughing filled my ears. Giselle was in the middle of it, directing the entire campaign. How brilliant she is! If she were a man she would no doubt have made a great general. Napoleon would be no match for her.

Good smells from the kitchen drew me in. I found Mrs. Flett serving bowls of her wonderful lamb stew to the men. Thankfully I am starting to understand her heavy dialect better each day. The moment I entered, she set a place for me at the long kitchen table and ladled a bowl of stew for me, accompanied by a hunk of her homemade bread. I thanked her with a smile and a nod.

As I ate, various men came in looking to be fed. They tipped their caps to me politely and left with their bowls of stew. All of them were very respectful except for one young man in his twenties who actually winked at me. He was clearly related to the others but was somehow more striking.

I am sure I blushed. No man has ever winked at me before.

Mrs. Flett scolded him angrily. She expressed her disapproval in such a loud and agitated manner that this time her words were lost to me. I caught that she called him Riff, though.

"Don't you mind him," Mrs. Flett told me once he was gone. She had calmed down enough that I could understand her once more. "Riff be a scoundrel."

I retreated to my room and continued to read until I noticed that the soft "summer dim" had replaced the day's light. It was lovely to read bits and pieces of how my father and mother had met at a café in Ingolstadt and fallen in love. But this romance was related only in side notes, as if they were an afterthought. What was really obsessing my father was the question of how to animate lifeless matter. He wasn't alone in this quest either. It was, apparently, the subject of great debate in public forums. Scholarly articles were being written about it. The subject was the cause of violent rifts among students and academics. My father was no madman. He was simply in tune with the concerns of his time.

After several hours, hunger induced me once more to put down the fascinating volume and seek food. As I descended the stairs, I noticed that the earlier clamor had turned silent. When I reached the first floor, I saw Giselle asleep in a high-backed chair she'd purchased from a local carpenter. The day's labors had clearly exhausted her.

On the large table in the kitchen, I found a plate of still-warm sausage-and-potato pie awaiting me. There was no sign of Mrs. Flett, so I assumed she had retired to her room for the evening. The one thing she hadn't left for me was something to drink, and so I began to search the kitchen. I recalled seeing Mrs. Flett come back from the market with a jug of apple cider and hoped I could find it among the pantry items.

After rummaging without success through the cabinets, I opened a closet door and peered into darkness before I realized that it was some sort of basement. Once my eyes adjusted, I saw the glint of jar lids and decided it must be a root cellar and that Mrs. Flett had already laid in some supplies. Perhaps she'd put the cider down there to keep cool.

Before descending the steps, I retrieved the lantern Mrs. Flett had left burning on the table. By its glow, I cautiously made my way down the narrow stone stairway. Just as I had thought, there were jars of pickled foods, barrels of potatoes, bags of flour, crates of nuts, and various other items Mrs. Flett must have purchased for our meals over the last several weeks.

The sound of scampering feet made me freeze, and I swept my lantern toward the scratching. Fortunately it was not a rat but a field mouse that faced me. I saw that he'd eaten clear through a burlap sack of flour. In the next second, he scurried off and I watched as he disappeared into the far wall. But a second look told me that it was not a wall but rather a door that the tiny rodent had squeezed under.

Hurrying to it, I tried the heavy iron bolt. It wouldn't budge, even though I threw all my weight into it. Further inspection revealed that a piece of metal blocked the movement of the bolt's bar. A key was required to open it.

What could be in there? Eager to know, I turned and let out a startled cry as I found myself facing Mrs. Flett.

"Sorry to scare you," I believe she said in her heavy dialect.

"Do you have the key to this door?" I asked.

She shook her head, glancing down at the heavy ring of keys she carried attached to the leather belt of her apron. "I was going to ask the same of you. No key I've been given opens this door."

Placing my hand on the door, I realized it was quite cool. "I will ask Uncle Ernest when he returns," I assured her as we walked out of the dark basement pantry together.

When we had climbed the stairs and were once again in the kitchen, Mrs. Flett warmed my meal further and, at my request, found the cider. "Mrs. Flett, do you know anything about our neighbor, Walter Hammersmith?" I asked as I ate. I meant to ask this casually, as idle conversation. In truth I was hoping she would have something to tell me. Since meeting him, I found he was constantly on my mind. I couldn't stop picturing his riveting gaze or hearing the low deep tone of his voice.

Mrs. Flett fixed me with a searching look. My attempt to conceal the keenness of my interest hadn't fooled her. "I know he rides that white horse of his at night," she said.

"But he can't walk," I told her.

"He walks well enough to get onto that mare," Mrs. Flett insisted. "I've seen him on it."

"Where does he go?"

"I don't know. The woman who shops and cleans for him says he's surly."

"I'm sure his condition makes him very unhappy," I speculated.

Mrs. Flett grunted dismissively, as though she were disinclined to grant Walter that much leeway.

When I finished, I went outside to walk a little before going to bed. In the deep dusk I spied Giselle standing near the edge of the cliff, her hair and dress blowing in the ever-constant wind. I was glad she was awake, since I hadn't spoken to her all day.

Although it was not entirely dark, a three-quarter moon had arisen. She seemed to be gazing at it.

"A beautiful night, isn't it?" I said as I came alongside her.

When she didn't turn or answer, I took a second, harder look at her. Her face was wide-eyed.

"Do you think he will come again?" she asked me.

"Who will come again?" I asked.

Giselle scowled deeply. "The man who came in the moonlight. The very bad man."

"What bad —" And then I realized she was asleep. She must have risen from her place on the chair and walked out here, still in a dream.

"There is no man, Giselle," I assured her.

"There is," she said confidently. "He tried to take me away. We must watch for him. I think he will come back and try again."

"Try to do what?"

"To take us."

"Take us where?"

Giselle suddenly whirled toward me, clutching my shirt by the collar. "We can't let him take us!" she cried. She dropped her head onto my shoulder and began to tremble. "He can't take us. He's bad!"

Wrapping my arms around her, I held tight. "No one will take you, Giselle. I promise."

Giselle made no reply but continued to shiver fearfully.

"Let's go in," I suggested, turning her toward the castle.

"Yes, we must go inside," she agreed. "It's safer there."

As I turned, I glanced over the cliff at the dark churning ocean below and saw a white horse cantering along the beach, Walter Hammersmith in the saddle. On horseback I would never have realized he was infirm. I wondered what he was doing riding alone on the beach at night.

He intrigues me so. I resolve to get over my shyness and go back to his house sometime very soon.

June 19

Right after breakfast this morning I made good on my resolution to see Walter again. With Mrs. Flett's help, I loaded a basket with some of the fresh eggs, butter, and milk that she buys from our neighbors. With these stowed, I donned my bonnet and shawl and headed for his cottage.

There were no white puffs of smoke coming from his chimney, but the weather was getting warmer every day and it was very possible that he'd chosen not to make a fire. When I knocked, there was no immediate response, but I knew it would take him a while to answer. With my ear to the door, I listened for the sounds of movement and heard nothing. Just as I was about to leave, I heard a scrape. It was as though someone had moved a container across a table. With this encouragement, I rapped on the door yet again. Still no one answered.

Then it occurred to me that perhaps he had fallen and needed help. Going around the corner, I saw that his horse was still there, docile as ever and munching grass. The windows were heavily curtained, but this time one corner of the curtain had fallen aside, enabling me to peer in.

Walter sat in the darkened room at a writing table. He was illuminated by the flame of a single candle. By its light I saw that he was slumped there with his head dropped into one hand. Never before had I witnessed a scene of such utter dejection.

Still worried that he needed help, I knocked on the window. This caught his attention, and slowly he gazed up at me. Scowling, he waved me off in a way I would have found rude were I not so concerned about his well-being.

Returning to the front of the cottage, I pounded on the door once more. "Lieutenant Hammersmith! Are you all right?"

The slow shuffle of his footsteps told me he was approaching. Soon I heard the lock opening. The door creaked open.

"Please go," he said, returning to his table. "I am not well today."

Feeling strangely bold, I entered the cottage, placing my basket on the table. "You should not be alone if you are ill," I insisted. "What bothers you?"

Tossing back his dark curls, he laughed bitterly. "What does not?"

I gazed at him with a questioning expression, which made him respond with more unhappy laughter. "My dear Fräulein Frankenstein, my wounds in conjunction with my mysterious disease of the nervous system have combined to make me a hopeless wreck," he said. "Of the many things that afflict me, an overwhelming sense of *despair* is probably my most acute and debilitating condition."

"You are deeply sad," I said. "I can see that."

"It's evident, is it?" he scoffed.

"Is it because you are in pain?"

"I awake with pain and sleep with it. Pain is my most intimate companion. But today my dark mood is worse than at other times. When this morose state comes over me I never can predict how long it will last."

"Perhaps it would be distracting if I read to you," I suggested, gesturing toward the many books on his shelves.

He looked me over, his brows furrowed in thought. "Perhaps it would," he allowed at last.

Outside, the patch of blue sky through the open door sparkled in stark contrast to the gloom within. "We could sit outside. It's a beautiful day," I said.

Squinting his eyes as though unaccustomed to the daylight, he shook his head. "That might bring on more good cheer than I am up to right now," he replied.

"You should smile more often," I commented. "It suits you." He was, indeed, very handsome when he smiled.

"I used to smile more often," he said, growing serious once more. "As you might imagine, I have seen better days."

"Perhaps you will see them again," I offered.

Walter shook his head. "This disease progresses in fits and starts, but it inevitably worsens with time."

"And science progresses every day."

"Are you always so optimistic?" he asked with a hint of sarcasm.

"I couldn't say. I only know that science is moving forward every day and it can do amazing things."

"Really?" he said, and I sensed he was mocking me.

"May I ask you a question?" I asked.

"That depends on the question," he replied.

"I saw you riding your horse the other day. How are you able to do that?"

"As you can see, I can still move around on my own a bit. My horse is old and sweet. I've had her since I was a boy, and she is patient as I fumble my way into the saddle. I was once a very adept horseman."

"Where do you go?"

"That's two questions." Lieutenant Hammersmith rose unsteadily. "Choose any book you'd like and we can read."

Surveying his books, I selected one called *Kinder- und Hausmärchen*.

"*Grimms' Fairy Tales*?" I asked. It was oddly out of place among his collection of military history and battle strategies. "It surprises me that you have this book."

"I read it completely when it was first published. Not for children at all. Much too frightening. But taken as a collection of folk stories, it is fascinating."

"Did you read it in German?" I asked.

"I did. It would have been easier for me in English, but I don't like to trust translations done by others. I prefer to translate for myself. I studied German in school."

"Would you like me to read it?"

"Yes. Its gloom and misery will be just the thing. Plus I will be interested to hear a native German speaker read it." He smiled after this statement, and I smiled back. I spent the next several hours reading in a wooden chair beside Walter while he listened from his corner.

At one point he reached out with his good left hand and took hold of mine. Startled, I looked at him. But his eyes were closed and his head leaned back in the chair.

His hand was large and warm. The sensation of having my own hand enfolded in his was lovely. It occurred to me to lean over and kiss his lips. I imagined that if I did so, he would pull me to him to kiss me back tenderly.

I became so lost in this daydream that my speech faltered. Checking him, I saw he had fallen asleep.

I gazed at his face, so wonderfully strong and manly in repose. It was his bitterness that occasionally warped the fine male beauty of his features. I sat and watched him slumber for a while, picturing him as he must have been when in better health. Finally, setting the book aside, I left quietly.

I think we have become friends. But I would love to be so much more to him.

CHAPTER TWELVE

FROM THE DIARY OF

BARONESS GISELLE FRANKENSTEIN

June 25, 1815

At last the day came for us to travel to Edinburgh, and Ingrid and I set out for the dock having sent our bags ahead in a cart driven by the arrogant Riff. He offered to take us but I declined, saying we preferred to walk. Now that Johann has returned, the man's charms don't hold the same power to thrill me that they once did, and I was glad to be in the open air with only my sister by my side.

I'd written to Uncle Ernest and he replied that he was eagerly awaiting us in Edinburgh and would happily chaperone my meeting with Johann. Ingrid, however, was not as happy about this meeting and made no disguise of her disapproval. "I don't trust him," she said in that overly candid way of speaking she can adopt from time to time as we walked along, nearing the harbor. "He was brutal to you. Forget him!"

"Stop saying that," I insisted. "You've made your feelings perfectly clear, but it's advice I can't take because my heart won't allow it."

"Does emotion rule you entirely?" she challenged.

"When it comes to Johann, it does," I confirmed, raising my voice to be heard above the wind.

"Well, don't let it," she insisted. "Use your intellect to overrule it. You deserve better than Johann."

"You don't understand, Ingrid," I replied. "You've never been in love like I have."

To my utter surprise, she blushed as deep a scarlet as I have ever seen her blush before. "*Have* you been in love?" I inquired quietly.

We had reached the harbor, where the tethered boats thumped against their moorings and screaming seabirds circled overhead. In this din I missed Ingrid's quick reply and without saying more, her face lit with interest at something she suddenly noticed. Turning from me, she ran toward a white horse that was tied to a post.

I hurried after her and when I reached her side she told me it was Lieutenant Hammersmith's horse. After speaking softly to the gentle creature, Ingrid then accosted a man working at the dock, asking why the horse was there. The man said that Lieutenant Hammersmith had taken his sailboat out that morning, though he didn't know where he'd gone to. "He can sail?!" she cried, seeming most surprised.

"Once he gets into the boat, he's fine," the man confirmed.

"He's a remarkable person," Ingrid said, and from the distant glaze in her eyes I couldn't tell if she was speaking to me or to herself.

"Is he?" I questioned. "From what you tell me, he simply sounds self-pitying and reclusive."

"Oh, no, you're wrong," she came back quickly. "He is a man of real depth and feeling. Despite his condition he still rides and sails. How many others with his afflictions would push themselves to do that?"

"You know him better than I do," I conceded. Was it the thought of Walter Hammersmith that had made her turn so crimson when I mentioned love? I hoped not. A dour crippled man leading a reclusive life in a thatched cottage was not the kind of mate I would wish for my sister. But I suspect she goes to see him quite often; I can tell when she's been there because of the faraway, dreamy look that comes over her. This can't be good for her; surely a romance with this man will not lead to the full life of the mind in stimulating society that she wished for, but would be more like a jail sentence.

"Have you fallen in love with Walter Hammersmith?" I asked, relying on my privileged position as her twin as an excuse for my directness.

Ingrid's panicked expression made her look like a trapped animal. With darting eyes, she seemed to be casting about for a way to escape me.

"Well, have you?" I pressed.

Ingrid walked off several paces and turned away from me. "It's madness, I know," she said. "But I can't stop thinking of him and replaying our conversations over and over in my head. When I am with him I am just so happy."

"Happy in that miserable dark cottage?" I questioned.

Turning to face me, Ingrid nodded. "When we are alone together there, no place could be better."

Our conversation was interrupted by the arrival of the taciturn Captain Ramsay, who was as disagreeable as always. He scowled darkly as he beckoned for us to follow him to his boat without even a word of greeting. I don't know why he seems to dislike us so; perhaps because we are newcomers to the Orkneys, or maybe he sees us as wealthy, spoiled young women because we dress well and have manners.

We made the crossing in silence, feeling too uneasy to converse in front of him.

Captain Ramsay said not a word to either of us, but then as we were disembarking, he muttered something. Although his thick dialect is nearly indecipherable, I suspect that what he said was quite rude and maybe even of an unsavory nature. I shot him a look of indignation, which he returned with a hard stare. I thoroughly dislike the man and hope we can find someone else to take us on the return voyage.

We got to the main island just in time for the ferry over to the town of John o' Groat's on the Scottish coast. Ingrid was scarcely there at all, she was so lost in her thoughts of Lieutenant Hammersmith. She nearly walked up the wrong gangplank on the ferry dock and might have ended up on the boat to Norway had I not run to redirect her.

As we crossed the water, I advised her once more to forget about Walter Hammersmith and think about someone more fun and suitable for her, like the young man she was about to see. Ingrid had recently received a letter from a fellow student named Anthony Verde with whom she'd become acquainted while she was in Lombardy. Although she insists there is nothing between them other than friendship and a collegial passion for science, she was most excited to learn that Anthony has enrolled in the University of Edinburgh, which has one of the oldest and most prestigious medical schools in the entire United Kingdom.

Needless to say, they refuse to admit women, but Anthony has promised to give Ingrid a tour of the school including the medical laboratories and, if possible, to smuggle her into his anatomy lecture, though for that she must dress as a man.

June 26

I am in love with the beautiful old city of Edinburgh with its ancient castle fortress on a high hill in the center of town. Stately neoclassic buildings from the middle of the 1700s surround the older part of town, which dates back to the year 1300. The city is no museum piece, though. It is as thriving and busy a city as any.

This morning Ingrid left our hotel in the old part of town to meet Anthony Verde with some of our uncle's clothing stuffed in a large bag. For a moment he questioned if he should let her go off with a young man unchaperoned. This made Ingrid laugh. "It can't harm my reputation since I'll look like a boy," she said. "And Anthony is the sweetest young man; there is no need to worry about him."

Luckily, our uncle is so focused on his business interests that he hasn't really been paying much attention to our comings and goings. This has allowed us considerable freedom which we never knew with our grandfather.

For Ingrid's sake, I hope this Anthony does have more than friendship in mind and will divert her from thoughts of our sickly neighbor, Lieutenant Hammersmith. I recall she once wrote me that Anthony was quite good-looking. The ways of attraction are certainly mysterious.

I am eager to hear how her day at the medical school is progressing, but now I must ready myself to meet Johann.

When he sees the woman I have become, he will be unable to resist me.

CHAPTER THIRTEEN

FROM THE JOURNAL OF

INGRID VDW FRANKENSTEIN

June 26, 1815

What a day I am having with Anthony! He has gone off momentarily to ask a friend something about his class here at the medical college of Edinburgh and has left me here at an outdoor table. I am using the time to make this entry in my journal.

It was good to see my old friend. He is, as always, lively and handsome with his dark, soulful eyes. It was so generous of him to give me a tour of the medical school. We shared great hilarity over my disguise as a male student. I can assure you I looked utterly ridiculous with Uncle Ernest's large trousers belted under my armpits and his hat down over my ears. It drew quite a few quizzical glances from Anthony's fellow medical students. It was all we could do to keep from bursting into gales of laughter.

The high point was by far the anatomy lecture. How I envy him the chance to sit in on these demonstrations! There with about fifty other students, I sat on an ascending set of wooden benches and looked down upon a real human body! A corpse, to be exact.

The cadaver was slit down the middle so that the heart and lungs were exposed. At first I found this shockingly gruesome and turned away in revulsion. But, quite honestly, it was only a matter of minutes before my fascination bade me return to the sight. From then on I could not look away. I was so keenly aware of what an opportunity this was.

The surgeon-lecturer lifted the heart right up from the body and held it out for all to see. He pointed out the valves and explained their workings. The corpse must have been newly deceased, for when he squeezed the heart, blood gushed from a slash in each of the wrists.

After the class, Anthony pulled me into a doorway of the medical school and handed me a package wrapped in burlap. "I smuggled it from the medical library for you," he whispered. "You must swear to return it when you have finished studying it. It's not theft as long as I return it."

"I swear," I promised excitedly. I began to open it, but Anthony gripped my arm.

"Not here," he warned. "Someone might see you."

Clutching the book to my chest, I thanked him. Leaving the university, we walked to a shop filled with students buying dried sausages, smoked fish, breads, and other food items for their lunch. We bought a loaf of bread, some cheese, and two apples for our lunch and then went to sit on one of the outdoor benches set up to the side of the store. "I've never seen a dead body before," I said as we ate. "How does the school come by them?"

A wary, guarded look came over Anthony's face.

"They claim that all the cadavers are from people who have donated their bodies to science," he said in a hushed tone. "But there is some question about that."

"What kind of question?" I asked.

"My classmate swears he recognized one of the bodies as belonging to a beggar who lived under a bridge."

"Are you saying he was killed so that they could use his body?"

Anthony shrugged, which I interpreted as a *yes*.

"Would the university do such a thing?" I asked.

"Not the university itself," Anthony said, leaning closer. "But there are men who make a living providing cadavers to medical schools. Since Edinburgh has one of the largest, they tend to congregate in the area."

A chill ran up my spine at the very thought of it. "Are you saying that Edinburgh is full of murderers?"

"Some are just grave robbers," he allowed.

"Just!" I cried, and then clapped my hand over my mouth. "That's bad enough," I added in a whisper.

"Others simply stay near the hospitals and charnel houses for the poor. They pretend to be family and claim the bodies of those who die with no one to bury them."

"That's terrible," I said.

"Yes and no," Anthony equivocated. "Murder is bad, yes. But using the bodies of those who are already dead to benefit the living . . . I think it can be all right. That is why the university *looks the other way*, as they say. It is for the greater good, and no one is hurt by it."

"I suppose," I said, even though I couldn't get over the feeling that it was a sort of desecration to those who had died and not intended for their bodies to be donated.

"Listen, my friend," Anthony went on, brightening. "You come tomorrow and I will get you into the lecture on guts."

"The intestines?"

"Yes. You will love it when they start taking out the intestines. They never stop coming."

"It sounds fascinating," I said.

Anthony began tapping my hand with rapid intensity. "Look! Over there, Ingrid!" He directed my gaze out to the street. "That man with the dirty hat and jacket, the one with the long blond hair."

I spied the disheveled man. "What about him?"

"They say he is a grave robber, and I myself have seen him making deliveries of large, human-sized bundles at the back door of the school's laboratories."

"What's his name?" I inquired.

"Gallagher."

I peered at the man and thought he seemed quite disreputable. Was I looking at a real murderer, a grave robber, or merely a man who haunted the hospitals awaiting opportunity? Whatever his degree of criminality, it was chilling to be so close to such a person. It was hard to believe that a man like Gallagher would be walking freely in the daylight. I would have imagined him staying strictly to the shadows and cover of night.

As though he sensed our gaze upon him, Gallagher turned his head sharply in our direction and stared at us. His glare was so sinister it sent a chill through me and I looked away. When I glanced back, he was gone.

Anthony appeared as shaken as I felt. "He provides a service," he said after a moment or two. "I try not to think about it too much."

"That's probably the wisest approach," I agreed.

CHAPTER FOURTEEN

FROM THE DIARY OF

BARONESS GISELLE FRANKENSTEIN

June 26, 1815

Today was warm enough to wear my blue silk traveling suit, the one with the empire waist and long jacket. Our hotel room has a fire in which I was able to warm my hair curling tongs, so I could frame my face in curls and form a few ringlets at the sides. Satisfied that I looked my best, I met my uncle, who has his own room at the end of the hall. After complimenting me on my beauty, he walked with me to the restaurant where Johann and I had agreed to meet.

I was grateful that Baron Frankenstein escorted me through the winding and hilly streets of the medieval center of Edinburgh. More than once the low heels of my boots caught in the uneven

Belgian blocks that make up the old roadways, and if my uncle's arm had not been there to catch, I might have stumbled. Moreover, Baron Frankenstein was a dear and stayed with me at the restaurant as we waited for Johann to arrive. The place was lovely, all dark carved wood, mirrors, leaded glass, crisp white linen tablecloths, and lit candles in iron sconces. The clientele was refined and the waiters dressed in white shirts with black pants under their aprons.

"I am so glad to see you again," I told him sincerely as we sat sipping tea. It surprised me how fond I'd become of my uncle, yet it was true. I had missed his protective presence while he was away.

"And I you. Your health has improved since last I saw you," Baron Frankenstein observed.

"You are right, I am happy to say," I agreed. "Though when the nights are windy and wet, I still feel congested. It is worst when I lay down to sleep."

"It can be a rough climate," Baron Frankenstein said. "Although temperate, it is damp and the wind is like nothing I have seen anywhere else."

The wind had become even more severe of late, and I found its intensity unnerving sometimes. It wasn't always easy to recognize where the roar of the ocean ended and the wail of the wind began. To step out of doors was to surrender oneself to a restless world of crashing waves and rustling leaves; the wind ran across the pasture grasses, moving them as though some invisible creature was parting the greenery. One's clothing and hair were constantly buffeted by an unseen hand.

"The wind clogs my ears and gives me bad dreams," I admitted to Baron Frankenstein.

A worried expression washed over his face, and when I inquired what was concerning him, he asked if I'd experienced further episodes of walking in my sleep. I assured him that I had not. I didn't elaborate on my nightmares, so as not to worry him, but I am starting to believe that the rattling and clanking of the wind pounding against the antique stones of the castle somehow gets into my mind and agitates it. Since arriving in Orkney, my dreams are the strangest I have ever experienced: I dream I am places I have never seen, talking to people I have never met.

Sensing someone's eyes on me, I glanced at the doorway and there I spied Johann. My heart leapt at the sight of him with his tall, strong physique, thick blond hair, and handsome face. As he approached, Baron Frankenstein prepared to depart, promising to meet me back at the hotel. Clearly he was eager to be off to his business meeting and that was fine by me since I longed to have Johann all to myself.

Johann and Baron Frankenstein exchanged quick cordialities and my uncle then left.

"Giselle, you are more gorgeous than ever," Johann said after kissing my hand and taking a seat beside me. "Being a baroness suits you."

It surprised me that he knew of my title, but then I recalled I had mentioned it to Margaret, my friend back in Ingolstadt.

"Do you think so?" I responded coyly. "In what way does it suit me?" This was of course a shameless ploy to elicit compliments from him, but I wanted to hear what he would say. I wanted to hear all the sweet words I had so longed for back in the very recent past when I had hoped he would love me, when I had hung on his every small expression of interest or the merest smile.

"It may be the fresh air, but were your eyes always such a vivid violet blue as they are now?" Johann inquired.

"I don't think they have changed." It was hard to be casual when I was so excited to see him, but it was important not to seem overly eager, especially after the way I had previously embarrassed myself.

Johann leaned closer to me and smiled. "Then it must be the time that has passed. You are now seventeen, are you not? You have turned a corner and become more womanly somehow."

"I can't imagine that being seventeen by only two weeks should make such a difference in one's appearance or demeanor," I protested.

"Yes, but I have not seen you in a month's time, since you upset everyone with your abrupt departure. Before you left, I thought of you as being much younger than I am."

"I am only two years younger than you," I reminded him.

"Two years is a good age difference between a man and a woman." Johann clutched my hand while gazing into my eyes with a deeply earnest expression. Then he drew me forward until our faces were very close. "Giselle," he murmured.

Feeling certain he would kiss me, I let my eyelids drift downward and then close softly as his lips brushed mine. The pleasure of it was so lovely that I melted toward him, resting my hand on his arm: It was hard to believe that the moment I had so often dreamed of was happening at last.

Slowly, he drew back. "Forgive my boldness, but you have grown so womanly, Giselle, that I am quite overwhelmed at the sight of you. You were always a beautiful girl, but you have become the most ravishing woman."

"Thank you, Johann," I replied in a dreamy tone, not removing my hand from his arm. "You are kind to say so."

"It is not kindness but sincerity."

I ate up this flattery as though his admiration were a kind of sweet food I had been starved for. To be sitting alone in a restaurant with such a good-looking suitor made me feel sophisticated and — yes, I must admit it — beautiful. And although of late I have attracted the attentions of passing men, I have never before been so gallantly declared to be *ravishing*.

As our eyes met, I was transported back to the time when I had once desired his love and esteem more than life itself. I didn't care if his behavior might be considered improper. To me, it was as if we were in a world all our own.

"I feel that you love me still, Giselle," Johann said softly. "Say it is so and you will make me happy, for I am consumed with my love for you. If you meant your absence to make me wretched, it has indeed. I have missed you every hour of every day."

My powers of critical thought seemed to have slipped beneath the surface of some sea of love and all I could do was take Johann at his word.

"Tell me you still love me," he urged. "I adore you and was a fool not to see it sooner."

At this I dropped my eyes, avoiding his gaze, unsure of how to compose my facial expression because the sheer happy delight I must have emanated was not the womanly aura I wished to project. Sliding my hand from his arm, I suggested that we should order our food.

"You're trembling," he noted tenderly.

"It's only hunger," I lied. In truth his nearness, his voice, his touch had left me shaken, feeling vulnerable and unsure of what to say or do next. There was no mistaking the emotion: I was once more as completely consumed by Johann as I had been before.

We ordered a lunch of lamb chops and potatoes, and while we ate, Johann did most of the talking. He told me how much he wanted to travel, that leaving Germany for the first time had kindled his appetite to see the world.

"We could go together, Giselle," he suggested with avid enthusiasm. "Your castle could be our starting point for exploring all of Scandinavia. Maybe we would go from there to Russia — perhaps even experience the Orient. We'd have to be married, of course."

"Married?" Had he really just used that word?

"Naturally. Imagine what a beautiful wedding we could have at the castle on the ocean!"

I easily pictured the gala reception since I had been envisioning my wedding day for as long as I could remember, even knew what my frothy white gown and billowing veil would look like. But all my life I had imagined that the man who asked me to marry him would be on bended knee, speaking beseechingly as he held forth a dazzling ring.

"Such a wedding might be too time-consuming, though," he said. "I think we should marry quickly. We could return to Edinburgh and be married by a judge, or even an itinerant minister if you prefer."

"What would be the reason for haste?" I asked.

"The sooner we're married, the sooner we can begin our life together. Imagine me, the lord of a castle on the ocean, married to a beautiful, smart, entrancing baroness! Not too bad for the son of a lawyer to become a member of the nobility."

"I find your suggestion somewhat pragmatic," I said. Was this what he was after — my castle and my title?

"Forgive me, Giselle! I was simply swept away with my visions of our happy life together. Of course I should not have presumed you would marry me, but you have always been fond of me, have you not?"

It suddenly irked me that — despite my previous declaration — he was so sure of himself, so confident that I would melt into his arms.

"I have liked you well enough," I said. "But life has changed."

"I know it has changed," he said. "You are now a baroness, a woman of independent fortune, and you need a husband to share it with."

"Do you believe that *someone* should be you?" I asked, surprised by the coldness I heard creeping into my voice.

"A woman needs a husband to help manage her affairs," he replied.

"And to spend her money?"

This remark was met with silence and an expression I could not interpret. A frost came into his eyes, causing me to think I had angered him. Fear of what angry words he would utter next made my heart quicken as I felt my shoulders lift, preparing for a battle of unpleasant words. I was relieved when he smiled suddenly.

"Let's discuss this further as we stroll," he suggested.

"You're not angry?" I asked.

"You have misunderstood me."

"I don't think I have," I said in a straightforward manner. "I once made a declaration of love that you rebuffed. Now word of my fortune has made you change your mind."

I was suddenly seized with a great desire to be away from him. I was filled with humiliation at being so used.

"I can make you see it a different way if you will only walk with me awhile," Johann insisted. "I have come all this distance, and I think you owe it to me to hear me out."

"I owe you nothing and resent your presumption."

"Giselle, did you not tell me to come meet you here? I came on this long journey at your invitation, and I believe that means you owe it to me to let me tell you how I feel. I have clearly done a bad job of it, but you must believe that is only because I am nervous at the thought of your rejection."

His words angered me, though I supposed he made a point — I *had* told him to come, never dreaming his goal was to woo me away from my new inheritance. I decided to put up with him for just a little longer. There could be, I thought, no hurt in that.

"Perhaps we can walk in the direction of my hotel, and that way you can escort me back," I proposed. "I'd appreciate it, since I do not know the city at all, but I do have the address of the hotel written on a paper in my purse."

"Surely you don't want to return there straightaway?"

"Yes, I do," I said as I extracted the slip containing the address. "Here's where we must go."

Johann slipped the paper in his jacket pocket and signaled the waiter for the check. "I know how to get there."

There seemed to be nothing more to say. It was a relief to finally reach the outside where the noises of the street distracted from the silence between us and where there were passing attractions — street performers and vendors — to casually remark upon.

As we walked, mostly in silence, I sneaked glances at him from the corner of my eye, and it occurred to me that Johann was not nearly as handsome as I had remembered him. How was it that I had never before noticed how close-set his eyes were or that there was a definite weakness in his jaw? There was a flare in his nostrils that gave his face an expression of arrogance that I had previously considered attractive, but no longer did.

After some distance, it seemed to me that we had walked for a longer amount of time than it had taken to arrive at the restaurant from the hotel. Also, I didn't recognize the deserted park into which we had wandered.

"Johann, are you lost?" I asked as we stopped by a narrow, winding river that looked as though it were man-made. "I am certain my uncle and I did not travel this way."

"Ah, you've caught me," Johann answered. "I knew if I could

only get you alone, I could change your mind about me." He took hold of my hand, and though I tried to draw it away, he held tight and used this grip to pull me toward him. Before I could protest, he had planted his lips on mine and was kissing me.

What I would have once longed for was now utterly repugnant to me. Pushing with all my strength, I made some distance between us.

"Johann! Stop it!" I cried.

"You love me, Giselle," he insisted, pulling me back to him, his hold tight. "You kissed me in the restaurant, and I could tell you enjoyed it."

"That was before I realized you were no more than a fortune hunter."

"A fortune hunter!" His face reddened with fury at my words. He gripped my wrist, twisting upward until it hurt. "Nobody calls me that!"

Grabbing my waist, he pulled me into a rough, wet kiss.

Biting his lip, I lurched away and searched the park unsuccessfully for another person to run toward. I ran from him but he quickly caught hold and was once more kissing me. I pried my arm from him and raked my fingernails across his face, drawing blood.

Infuriated, he called me a name I have never heard before and never want to hear again. With a quick, sharp blow, he knocked me to the ground, where we struggled until I was able to break loose and get to my feet. I lost all sense of myself, all sense of any thought but that of escape.

I ran blindly from the park through the quiet streets, looking over my shoulder to check if he was pursuing me but did not see him. Breathlessly, I climbed chipped narrow stone stairways leading back toward the center of town. At a busy thoroughfare, I finally recognized the way to the hotel and headed for it.

Oh, Diary, this is an event I want to wipe from my mind completely. Horrible! So horrible! Now that I have written about it I never want to think of it again.

CHAPTER FIFTEEN

FROM THE JOURNAL OF

INGRID VDW FRANKENSTEIN

June 26, 1815

My mood lifted as Anthony walked me back to the hotel. He told me of the surgeon who would give the lecture on the diseases of the colon and on how diseased sections of it could be simply cut out and reconnected with a special string made from catgut.

"The body is really quite mechanical when you break it into its components, isn't it?" I remarked as we neared the hotel.

"In its material components, it is all quite logical," Anthony agreed. "But what is that magical force that animates the flesh? That's the mystery. It is what I think of as God."

"Must it be so mystical?" I questioned. "God may watch over us and judge our morality, but is it necessarily divine intervention that starts life? Might it not be an electrochemical reaction such as any other? Whether sent by God or simply powered by itself."

"*Electro*chemical?" Anthony asked.

"Yes. You know I studied with Count Volta. I have continued reading works on electricity as it interacts with other chemicals," I said. I told him too that I had come upon my father's experiments and writing on this subject. I didn't say that I felt that my father had surpassed even Galvani and Volta in his findings. I didn't want to seem a boastful daughter. And I also did not want to delve too deeply into the circumstances of my father's life. I knew Anthony was ignorant of them, and I wasn't about to enlighten him.

"You should contact Jakob Berzelius," Anthony suggested.

I knew the name, and remembered that my father had been in touch with him. They had exchanged letters on the possibility of curing disease through the use of electric current.

"Is he still in Sweden?" I asked.

"He's teaching at a university there," Anthony confirmed. "I'll try to get more information for you."

At the front door of the hotel, Anthony stopped and took my hands in his. "Ingrid, we get along so well," he said. "And it is so good to see you again."

He lifted the man's hat I had worn all day, which allowed my hair to tumble loosely to my shoulders.

"I no longer look like a man," I said with a laugh.

"No, now you look like the lovely young woman you are," Anthony said, his dark eyes beaming affectionately. "Could you ever think of me as more than a friend?"

The image of Walter in his chair, with his eyes closed, his hand holding mine, flew unbidden into my head.

"Anthony, you are so dear to me," I began. "We do have fun together."

Immediately a look of disappointment came over him. "I'm sorry I spoke. You don't have the same feelings for me. I can hear it in your voice and see it on your face."

"I might feel otherwise if another had not already taken that place in my head and my heart."

"He's lucky. I hope he knows that."

"I'm not sure how he feels," I answered honestly. Perhaps he had only grasped my hand as he was falling asleep. It could have been a gesture of friendship. Nothing like that had happened since, although I had read to him other times. We had become deeply companionable, but no more.

"If he foolishly does not return your feelings, write to me and I will come to your side at once."

Squeezing his hands fondly, I promised I would. Anthony

would be a wonderful romance for me. He is handsome. Charming. And we have so much in common. But I could not lead him on with Walter constantly on my mind.

Anthony threw off the awkwardness and said he'd come for me in the morning. He would sneak me into the demonstration on intestines. I told him I couldn't wait, which was absolutely true.

"Is it safe to open my package now?" I asked.

"I suppose so."

With eager fingers, I opened the burlap and gasped with delight. It was Doctor William Harvey's *On the Motion of the Heart and Blood*. Gingerly I turned the yellowed, crumbling pages.

"Is this from the sixteen hundreds?" I guessed. I knew from my private readings that William Harvey had been the physician to King James. It was he who had disproven the existing theories of the day regarding circulation. Excitedly, I read from the page I had opened to: *The heart does not make blood, instead the same blood circulates endlessly around the body. It goes around and around without being absorbed, and the heart is simply the pump that sends it on its way.* Inside were the most detailed anatomical drawings. They were not as perfectly drawn as those in my father's papers, but they were easier to follow in their relative simplicity.

"Harvey was brilliant," Anthony said. "Even though this volume is almost two hundred years old, you will learn a lot from it. It is not available anywhere but in a medical library. You could not buy it anywhere, not with all your new fortune." He grinned, pleased to have given me such an invaluable treasure.

Still holding the book, I hugged him. "Oh, you are such a true friend. I can't thank you enough," I said sincerely. "I shall be up all night taking notes."

"No, my friend, sleep, so you can be alert for tomorrow's lecture," Anthony counseled.

"I'll try, but it won't be easy." Bidding him farewell, I entered the hotel's quiet lobby. But the day was still warm and my mind was so filled with everything that had happened today. And so I turned around and went for a walk to enjoy the last of it. Now I sit on a park bench in Parliament Square near the Cathedral of Saint Giles and write. I want to get it all written down before any of it leaves my head. This may be my only chance to write, because I know that once I get to my room I will be completely absorbed in Dr. Harvey's revolutionary work on the heart.

Even though I never knew him, I imagine that my father would have been proud of my inquisitiveness, and the lengths to which I've gone to investigate further.

CHAPTER SIXTEEN

FROM THE DIARY OF

BARONESS GISELLE FRANKENSTEIN

June 26 (continued)

My heart is torn apart and I am wretched beyond belief. This has been the most hideous day of my life. I feel like such a fool to have thought that Johann had truly changed in his feelings toward me when all the while he only loved the idea of gaining control of my fortune. Not only is he not the person I thought him to be, but he is a brute and a scoundrel. In a thousand years I could never have expected him to attack me as he did.

I shudder to think of what might have happened had I not been able to fight him off.

It was not easy to make my way home, since the attack had left my mind in complete disarray. On the way I passed police officers but did not think to tell them what had happened. In truth all I wanted was to be back safe in my hotel room.

When I finally made it back, I was disappointed that Ingrid had not yet returned. I longed to tell her what had happened. I noticed a note that had been slipped under the door and retrieved it. It was written in the hand of one of the hotel staff, saying that my uncle had sent word that he would not return tonight but rather stay with a friend some miles away.

As soon as I looked at my image in the full-length mirror, I was glad that neither my sister nor my uncle was there to see the state I was in. My hair was almost completely unpinned and there was blood all over me from a wound I incurred on my right hand. I have scrapes of all kinds.

An urgent desire for a bath suddenly consumed me, and I couldn't shed my bloodstained clothing quickly enough. The very idea that Johann's skin might linger under my fingernails repulsed me; I longed for every trace of him to be washed away.

The claw-foot tub in the bathroom was deep, and I lay in it for a while with a blank mind.

Another onslaught of tears overwhelmed me as I thought of Johann. I had learned to accept his disinterest in me, but to then raise my hopes with such callous motives was so unconscionable. What could he have been thinking by pressing himself on me like that? Did he believe that once he had robbed my virtue I would have no recourse but to marry him?

I wanted nothing more than to block it all from my mind, and so, shutting my eyes, I lay my head back against the back of the tub.

There was to be no escape, however, for in the next instance I was dreaming that Johann had me thrown over his shoulder and was carrying me into a shadowy forest of towering pines. I screamed, kicking and scratching, determined to squirm free from his viselike grip but unable to. In this dream my fear was completely unbridled, greater even than it had been today in the park. The sky shook with thunder as it opened, releasing a torrent of rain. Aware that I was losing my battle to break free of Johann, I screamed for help but was suddenly unable to breathe and started to choke. Then I heard Ingrid's voice calling to me as if from very far away.

My eyes snapped open, and I was, in fact, choking and sputtering because I had sunk just below the water's surface and must have cried out in my sleep, allowing the bathwater to flood into my open mouth.

Panicked, I sat bolt upright, gripping the tub ledge and coughing as though my lungs might burst.

"Giselle?" Ingrid called through the bathroom door.

I opened my mouth to reply, only to find my voice so choked with emotion that I could not steady it sufficiently to speak.

"Giselle! Shall I come in? What's wrong?" she kept on.

I didn't want her to see me so distraught and so found my voice enough to ask her to wait. I stepped out of the tub and wrapped myself in a robe.

Feeling overwhelmed, I sat a moment on the edge of the tub and fell into tears once again. Ingrid's expression was a mask of horrified concern when she stepped into the bathroom and found me sitting there.

CHAPTER SEVENTEEN

FROM THE JOURNAL OF

INGRID VDW FRANKENSTEIN

June 26 (continued)

When I went into our room about an hour later, I could see Giselle's clothing was tossed carelessly around the room. Her diary lay closed on her bed. It was not like her to be so slovenly.

"I'm back!" I called to the closed bathroom door.

A long period of silence was followed by the sound of Giselle coughing.

"Are you all right?"

Giselle's coughing continued. After a few minutes more, I rapped loudly on the door. "Giselle? Shall I come in? What's wrong?"

Cracking open the door, I saw that her head was in her hands as she sat propped on the edge of the tub. Her luxuriant hair veiled her face, but the lift and fall of her shoulders told me she was, indeed, weeping heavily. "Go away, please," she pleaded in a sob-choked tone. "I'll come out in a moment."

"All right," I agreed out of respect for her wishes. It wasn't easy since I wanted to race to her side to discover the cause of her unhappiness.

It had to have been Johann. I've always believed he was vain and unworthy of Giselle's tender affections. Everything she'd ever told me about Johann made me dislike him. Whenever I voiced this, she wouldn't hear of it. Where Johann was concerned, she made every allowance for his shallow self-centered behavior and his rudeness to her. I suppose it was an example of love's legendary power to render blind the one who is in love.

While I waited, I picked up the clothing Giselle had flung so recklessly. The white shirt she had worn beneath the jacket of her blue traveling suit was speckled with red. Lifting it to my nose, I detected the pungent, iron-tinged odor of blood.

As I was examining this, Giselle emerged from the bathroom wrapped in her thick, paisley-print robe. Her eyes were swollen from crying. "Giselle, what's happened?" I asked urgently, wrapping my arm around her.

She didn't answer until I'd gotten her seated on the bed. Giselle choked out the story of how she had thought Johann had come to her out of love but that over lunch it had soon become clear that he was only after her inheritance.

"Are you sure that's why he came?" I asked.

"I'm certain of it. He found out about the fortune from Margaret. He's already planning how he will spend it traveling the continent, and live at the castle when he's not traveling across the globe."

Giselle threw herself against my shoulder and fell into another fit of forceful crying. "And it gets worse!"

"What? Tell me!" I urged.

"He tried to force his affections on me, and when I rebuffed his advances, he hit me!"

"He hit you!" I cried, outraged. Pulling back, I examined her. When I brushed away her hair, I observed a definite blue-purple welt on her cheekbone. Checking her hands, I saw they were horribly scraped. One very pronounced gash across her palm was probably the source of the bloodstains on her shirt.

Filled with furious indignation, I stood. "Have you told this to Uncle Ernest?"

Giselle shook her head. "He sent a message that he is visiting a friend in Glasgow and won't return until tomorrow."

"Then *I* will go speak to Johann's father myself. He can't be allowed to get away with this. We'll have him arrested. Where are they staying?"

"I have no idea," Giselle replied, wiping her eyes.

"Then in the morning I will go to every hotel in search of them," I resolved. "I will check every register."

"It was horrible, Ingrid," Giselle sobbed.

Holding her tight, I rocked her soothingly until her breathing slowed. Lowering her to the bed, I pulled the covers over her and was glad she drifted quickly off to sleep.

A murderous rage consumed me. Needless to say, I did not spend the evening studying Harvey's book on the heart as I had planned. Rather, I sat in the dark seething, still fully dressed in my manly disguise.

How dare he attack my sister? How dare he!

June 27

When the first rays of dawn crept through the window, I couldn't wait any longer. I left our room and went out into the quiet streets determined to locate Johann and his father. In the half-light of early morning, my man's clothing made me feel less vulnerable than I would have felt in a dress.

Doggedly I went from one hotel to another, starting with the outer ring of the newer part working my way in toward the medieval section, asking after Johann and his father. My search went on for over an hour with no success. Finally, I came upon a narrow, dirty hotel with a threadbare green awning. The name ROOSTER'S CLAW INN AND TAVERN was scrawled in chipped paint across the front window. It seemed a disreputable establishment — not the sort of place Johann and his father would frequent. Just as I was turning away from it, though, a horse-drawn carriage came along the road and turned into an alleyway beside the hotel that was just barely wide enough for it to fit.

Could Johann and his father be sneaking out at dawn to avoid the police? I didn't want to let them slip away, so I turned down the alley, determined to have a look at what was going on.

When I rounded the corner, two men were standing at the back door of the hotel. Immediately I ducked back behind into the alley so they wouldn't see me. Surreptitiously I peered at them from around the corner of the building. Instantly my hand shot to my mouth to stifle a gasp. One of the two men was the sinister Gallagher. From this closer vantage he was even more frightening, with rotted teeth and pockmarked skin. His companion was equally alarming, of darker complexion and burlier. He had been the one driving the carriage on the way in.

In the next moment, the back door opened and a heavy man passed them a large package bundled in burlap and tied with rope. It was easily the size of a human body.

There was no conversation exchanged as Gallagher got into the coach and his associate perched atop the coachman's seat once more. I watched as they left by way of the alley on the opposite side of the building.

So there it was! I had witnessed a dead body taken away in the early hours of the morning. What would they do with it? Where would it end up? How much money would they receive?

I turned to walk back up the alley and immediately saw that my path was blocked by the very same coach. The men had gone around the front of the street and turned back in. As I pivoted to retreat around the other way, my motion was stopped by Gallagher, who stood blocking my way. I was trapped! Instantly I recoiled in fear and revulsion to the stench of body odor and alcohol that emanated from him.

Gallagher gripped my arm roughly and then grinned, displaying his decayed teeth. "You're a girl!"

I nodded, too frightened to speak.

"What are you doing here?" he demanded, his smile disappearing.

My lips seemed to be moving independently of my terror-frozen brain. I don't know where I found the wit to concoct the story I told him. "I'm a medical student. That's why I'm dressed as a man. So I can sneak into the medical school."

"A sneak, eh?" Gallagher said. "Nothing wrong with that. Why are you here?"

"Bodies," I said. "I need money, and I heard you could make some selling bodies to other medical students."

Gallagher shook me harshly. "And what made you think you could find a body here?"

"I heard things," I replied, working to keep my voice steady. "The medical students talk. They guess about where the cadavers come from."

"The dead donate their bodies to science," Gallagher sneered cynically.

"Yes, I know." It occurred to me that I might soon become one of those bodies. Gallagher seemed to be a man who could slit my throat and not think twice about it.

Gallagher eyed me up and down. "Are you strong?"

I nodded.

"You need money and I have a job needs doing. I have more corpses to claim, and I could use someone to help pull the bodies into the carriage and sit with them. Sometimes they get stiff and even look like they're sitting up. You got to knock the body down so nobody sees it. Can you do that? It would free my friend up there to help me with the heavy lifting."

It sounded awful. But I was fascinated. Besides, what would he do to me if I refused?

"All right," I said.

"If you tell anyone, I'll find you and kill you."

"I'll never tell," I assured him.

With a nod, he bade me to follow him into the carriage. I was almost knocked back by the smell of the rotting corpse. "And this one is only a few hours old," Gallagher said with a laugh. "Wait till we get a few that've been stewing for a while."

For the next hour we drove through the streets of Edinburgh collecting dead bodies. At the hospital we picked up two bodies. I waited at the dark end of a cemetery while Gallagher and his companion entered and returned covered in dirt with another burlap sack. I helped pull it into the carriage.

This body was so rank with decay that I had to lean out the window to vomit. This caused the two men to laugh uproariously. It was the first time I heard the other man make any sound at all.

It was almost fully light before they dropped me at a corner near my hotel. "It's better if you don't know where we're delivering these," Gallagher said as he paid me from a roll of money he took from his pocket. "You did good by us. If you ever want to work for me again, be at the Rooster Claw at the same time. And remember to keep your mouth shut."

Nodding, I took the money. "I know."

When I got back to my hotel room, Giselle still slept soundly. Bathing required me to scrub with an abundance of soap to rid myself of the odor that seemed to have seeped into my hair and skin, into my very skin. My man's clothing was now so foul that I had to dress and ask the concierge to admit me to Uncle Ernest's room for fresh clothing. (I claimed he had sent word requesting them.)

It was only then did it occur to me that I had failed in my mission to find Johann and his father. Guilt flooded me as I realized I had let Giselle's attacker escape due to my obsession with my own scientific pursuits. I had utterly failed my twin! I cursed my selfishness, but the moment to act had passed. Surely they had gone by now.

Soon I was once more dressed as a man and standing in front of the hotel, awaiting Anthony. Maybe I should have stayed back with the sleeping Giselle to tend to her, but I couldn't stand to miss this next lecture. Once more my ruthless pursuit of science was interfering with my sisterly duties. I was plagued with guilt, but it did not stop me. There was no telling when such a chance would arise again.

"You look fatigued, my friend," Anthony greeted me. "Were you up all night carousing?"

"You'll never believe where I've been," I told him. As we walked toward the medical school, I revealed all that had happened.

"That was very dangerous of you," he scolded.

"What choice did I have?" I countered.

"You should have contacted the police regarding this Johann. In that case, you would not have been out unescorted to begin with."

"I suppose so," I conceded.

That morning I once more sat riveted by the sight of a human body with its insides revealed. This day the surgeon lecturer cut out a section of colon and then reattached it. The skill with which he sewed the pieces of flesh together was no different than the way a tailor might connect a sleeve to a coat. I had been taught to sew. I could do this type of stitching.

I gazed down at the two cadavers on the tables. The one being stitched had a cloth over his face. The other was of an elderly woman who appeared as though she was only sleeping peacefully. Naturally I was reminded of my morning's adventure.

Did I feel guilty about it? Asking myself this important question, I waited for my innermost self to reply.

The true answer was no, I did not.

What did the dead care? They felt no pain or shame. If they had family who might have cared, their bodies would have been claimed.

Did I think all this because it eased my conscience? Because I wanted to think it?

I didn't care.

Glancing around the arena, I saw all the medical students furiously taking notes. I began to do the same.

By the time I returned home, Giselle was dressed and appeared to be completely returned to her old self. She was wearing a lovely flowered gown with a lace collar. Her Indian-print shawl was draped over her shoulders. She'd swept up her hair in a coiled, braided bun that was very becoming. Even the high-button boots, which had been dirty and scraped yesterday, now gleamed.

"Sister, how are you?" I asked, peeling off my man's jacket and stepping out of the tightly belted trousers.

With a critical eye, she took me in. "I'm fine. How are *you*? You look exhausted!"

"I found it impossible to sleep last night," I admitted. "Then, before dawn, I went out to find Johann and his father."

"You didn't!" Giselle gasped.

"I did. And you will never guess what happened to me."

When I opened my mouth to speak again, I was surprised to discover it was quite dry. My mind also was blank. Some inner impulse was stopping me from telling my twin about my escapade with the body snatchers. This was odd, since I usually told Giselle everything.

"What?" she prodded.

"I couldn't find them," I said. "Perhaps they've left town to escape prosecution. When Uncle Ernest returns, we'll enlist his help in going to the authorities."

"No, we won't," Giselle stated firmly. "I'm glad you didn't find them, and I don't want Baron Frankenstein to know of this. I couldn't bear it if anyone was to find out about this humiliation."

"Giselle, you can't let him get away with it. He hit you!"

Giselle's complexion went red with anxiety. "That's right, Ingrid, he hit *me*, not you. It's for me to decide how to handle this."

I was stunned. I don't think she has ever spoken to me so harshly.

"But, Giselle —"

"No! You must respect my wishes on this, Ingrid. I want to put this behind me as though it never happened, to block it from my mind completely. We will not speak of it or think of it again."

"How will we explain your injuries?" I asked.

"I tripped and fell."

"Is that truly what you think is best?" I questioned doubtfully.

"It is," she confirmed.

"There is nothing you wish to do? Not at all?"

"There is something," she replied.

"What?"

"I want to throw a party."

CHAPTER EIGHTEEN

FROM THE DIARY OF

BARONESS GISELLE FRANKENSTEIN

July 1, 1815

Along with Baron Frankenstein, we traveled by ferry from Scotland to the island they call Mainland and stayed at a hotel in the city of Kirkwall. From there we booked a trip to Gairsay with a boat taking groceries across, but at the last moment I was delayed as the clasp to my luggage broke and my clothing fell from it. They did not notice me frantically gathering my things until the boat had already left the dock.

This unfortunate turn of events left me with no choice but to engage the sailboat of that same taciturn Captain Ramsay for my return trip. I decided to simply remain aloof and not even look at him. Our journey would be over soon enough.

To my dismay, the old man was oddly talkative as we set sail. "So, tell me, girly," he began in his thick, growling way of talking. "Have you found yourself a lad over there in Gairsay?"

I thought his question impudent, and so declined to answer and avoided looking at him by gazing out to sea.

"Too good to speak to me?" he challenged.

"I can't hear you because of the wind," I lied, though I needed to shout to be heard, just the same.

"A loud little trollop, aren't ye?" he snarled.

I couldn't believe my ears, and so once more I feigned deafness, staring away from him. From time to time I checked to see what he was doing, and each time I was met with a hateful stare.

When the bay was in sight, the captain did not steer the boat into it but rather into a cove. I demanded to know where he was going.

"Never you mind!" Captain Ramsay replied as he headed into more shallow waters in a quiet, rocky inlet.

I couldn't imagine why we would be going there and grew frightened.

"Take me back!" I shouted, standing.

"Sit down," he bellowed.

"I WANT TO GO BACK!"

From his spot at the tiller, he reached forward and grabbed my skirt, yanking at it. The boat pitched, throwing me down onto him at the same time that the mainsail mast swung above us.

"Now look what you've done, you stupid girl!" he shouted, struggling to get to his feet and regain control of the boat.

The next thing I knew, we were in the water and the boat had capsized. My luggage was once more open and my things floating in the surf. Fortunately, you, Dear Diary, were safe in my pocket. You are damp and some ink is blurred, but you're not too much the worse for your drenching.

I did not look for Captain Ramsay, but quickly dragged myself out of the water, which was fortunately low enough that I could stand. Once I was knee-deep in the surf, I hobbled along in the direction of the harbor by hugging the shoreline. Fortunately it was a warm day, and by the time I got there, I was already half dry. I saw Ingrid and Uncle Ernest there waiting for me. Frantic with worry, they hurried to my side as soon as I came into view.

"We were planning to take the next boat back to get you," Ingrid said. "What has happened to you?"

"I came over with that awful Captain Ramsay and his boat overturned. He didn't pull into the bay but into an inlet."

"Perhaps he pulled in there because something was wrong with his boat," Baron Frankenstein suggested.

"I don't know. I stood in the boat and we argued, then the boat went over. I have left him to his own devices; he surely doesn't need my assistance."

"No, surely not," Baron Frankenstein agreed, wrapping his arm around my shoulder as he guided me up the hill away from the water. "Let us get you back to the castle so you can rest after such a fright."

A fit of coughing suddenly seized me, the same low hacking cough I'd experienced upon first coming to the island.

Ingrid was instantly at my side, her hand on my shoulder. "See? This is what I was worried about. This climate is too rough for you. All it took was a fall in the water to set you back."

I assured her I was fine, but was once again overcome by another spasm of coughing.

Once back up at the dock at Gairsay, we were met by Riff in the driver's seat of a horse-drawn cart. He had been sent by Mrs. Flett to pick up us and our things.

Ingrid needed Riff's assistance, since her friend Anthony has loaded her with anatomy and chemistry books he's "borrowed" from the Edinburgh medical library and loaned to her. Ingrid, with her typical taste for the gruesome and Gothic, also bought a novel in Scotland called *The Sargasso Manuscript*. She tells me it is about secret societies; cabalists; Gypsies, Muslims, and Moors; and even features a set of beautiful twin sisters.

For the first time, Riff saw us side by side and was clearly shocked by the realization that we were not one and the same. "There are two of you?" he cried in his thick Orkneyan cadence. "I just thought that some days you looked stunning and other days you were plain."

Immediately I checked to see how Ingrid was taking this thoughtless insult, hoping that she had not understood what he'd said.

I never quite know if Ingrid truly doesn't care about her appearance. As a twin, one must stake out one's own territory in order to thrive as an individual, and since I lack Ingrid's brilliance, perhaps she has generously left the looks as my concern.

Riff's callousness disturbed her, though: The blush that came to her cheeks told me so, and it hurt me to see how she turned away from him as though his words were actual barbs that had wounded her.

"Of course there are two of us, you dolt," I scolded angrily. "Any idiot who had been at the castle two minutes would know that."

As harshly as I delivered my reprimand, he didn't seem especially perturbed. He held me in his insolent, overlong stare that no doubt he used on every girl in Gairsay.

"Fiery when you're angry, aren't you?" he leered. "But you don't look so great today either. You're a bit of a wet hen yourself."

"Oh, be quiet, will you?" I shot back.

"That is quite enough from you, young man." Baron Frankenstein came to my aid. "Just take the packages to the castle, and we will follow on foot. Go!"

Still maintaining his infuriating smirk, Riff turned the wagon and left. "I will have Mrs. Flett dismiss that fellow immediately," Baron Frankenstein assured us.

"He is certainly full of himself, isn't he?" Ingrid commented, looking down at her hands.

"Forget about him," I told Ingrid, taking her hand as the three of us began climbing the road toward the castle. She nodded, though I could see that she was still smarting from the verbal slap.

By the time we got back to the castle, I wanted nothing more than to peel off my wet clothing and crawl into my bed.

Dear Diary, I am so glad this whole wretched trip is done at last.

CHAPTER NINETEEN

July 1, 1815

Attending Anthony's classes at the medical school has given me a fever for knowledge. It is so difficult to teach oneself! Frustrating! But this trip has advanced my understanding of anatomy a hundred times over. As soon as I got back to the castle, I settled on a couch and began writing this.

Giselle, poor thing, dashed away for a nap in her room. I fear that this trip was too hard on her, between her awful encounter with Johann and the boat accident with the disagreeable Captain Ramsay. She's begun coughing again, which is not a good sign.

But despite my worry, I checked to see if there was smoke

coming from Walter's chimney before we'd even reached the front door. There was, and I was relieved that he had made it back safely from wherever it was he'd gone off to in his sailboat. I admire how he manages to get about so well without the full use of his limbs.

I will stop writing now and peruse my medical books. They are the only things that can keep me from rushing over to see Walter. I don't want to seem like a love-struck girl who goes straight to see the object of her affection the moment she returns home.

Still, I wonder if he's missed me.

July 1 (continued)

Finally I couldn't wait to see Walter for another second. With an eager heart, I hurried across the grass to his cottage.

I don't know how long it was after knocking that I waited at Walter's front door. As much as I'd felt I couldn't confide in Giselle or Uncle Ernest about my exploits with the grave robbers, I was eager to tell Walter all about it.

Listening at the door, I heard no sound. When I went around the side, his horse was there and whinnied a greeting. I was pleased that she was becoming familiar with me. The curtains had been drawn shut again, so I could not see in. Rapping on the window failed to bring any result.

Wandering around the back, I discovered a kitchen door. It was unlocked and I let myself in.

"Lieutenant Hammersmith?" I called. "It's me, Ingrid."

Slowly I went deeper into the room and found Walter asleep in his chair. He'd thrown off half of the blanket that had been drawn over him, revealing his legs, or rather a leg and a half. His right leg had been amputated just below the knee. It was heavily bandaged and the wrappings were bloodstained.

Horrified, I backed out of the cottage as I had entered. How my heart ached for him! I could not begin to imagine what agony he'd undergone to have such an operation. What pain it must be causing him still!

Unwilling to wake him, I ran back to the castle. Hurrying up the winding staircase, I came straight to the room where my father stored his notebooks. It was the one place I knew I could be alone. Once there, I sat and cried until my eyes ran dry of tears. I fell asleep right there on the floor.

I dreamed I was back in Italy with Count Volta and Anthony. They were very excited about something, and I felt as though they had been waiting for me to arrive. They wanted to bring me to meet Luigi Galvani, to see his latest experiment. We went into a room and Walter was there with Galvani. He wore a hospital gown and seemed happy. In a second I saw that his legs had been replaced with human-sized frog legs. Galvani had him hooked to a battery and the wire that attached him to it crackled with electricity. Walter sprang high into the air on his new legs, laughing with delight. I had never seen him so filled with joy.

"You can make this happen if you have the key, Ingrid," Anthony said.

"What key?" I asked.

He pulled a large, ornate key from the pocket of his coat.

I awoke with a start, filled with inspiration. I was the daughter of Victor Frankenstein. Fate had brought me here to this isolated island for a reason. I, and I alone, would make a new man of Lieutenant Walter Hammersmith.

In my heart, I felt it was so. Yet was this key real or only metaphorical?

I have no way of knowing.

CHAPTER TWENTY

FROM THE DIARY OF

BARONESS GISELLE FRANKENSTEIN

July 1 (continued)

I napped for several hours and awoke feeling stronger, though the tickle in my throat persisted. I dressed and went down the stairs to find Ingrid and Baron Frankenstein. Ingrid was draped across a couch Mrs. Flett had purchased for us from one of her cousins, a furniture maker, reading one of the anatomy books Anthony had lent her. Baron Frankenstein was sitting at a desk, apparently writing a letter.

"How are you feeling?" he asked when he noticed me.

"Much better, thank you," I said. "When you post your letter, can you take a batch of my party invitations with you?"

"Certainly," he agreed.

Ingrid looked up from her book and fixed me in a curious gaze.

"What?" I inquired.

"Are you sure you're strong enough to throw this elaborate gala you have in mind?"

"Absolutely. This will be the most wonderful party," I replied. "These first invitations are only to people we know from home, in case they might be traveling or wish to make the long trip. I still have many more to write, and I'll need you to make a list of who you would like to invite. It doesn't matter if you know them or not; we will say we have extended the invitation because we so esteem their scientific achievement."

"Doubtless many will know of your late father," Baron Frankenstein added, "and they will be eager to meet his daughters."

"Do you really think so?" Ingrid asked, brightening at the prospect.

"Indeed," Baron Frankenstein affirmed.

"I long to speak with his colleagues," Ingrid said. "I have so many questions, and it is difficult to study by one's self."

"Might I ask you what you hope to gain in your pursuit of a medical education?" our uncle asked. "You know you will never be allowed to practice as a physician because of your gender."

"I don't want to be a doctor, Uncle Ernest," Ingrid answered. "Rather, I thirst for answers. How does life begin? What are its building blocks? Why are we alive at all? It's the unknown that intrigues me. Didn't Aristotle say that the unexamined life was not worth living?"

"It is certainly simpler," our uncle countered.

"Don't worry about me," Ingrid assured him. "I'll be fine."

Baron Frankenstein answered with a sigh.

"And what about you, Giselle?" Ingrid asked. "Are you also fine?"

"Perfectly well," I replied, and it was true. The only thing I wanted to think about was this party and how wonderfully elegant it would be. It would be the official start of our new lives.

Ingrid stood, clutching her science book to her chest. "If you'll excuse me, I really want to concentrate on these books from Anthony."

"Certainly," Baron Frankenstein said. When Ingrid was gone, he turned to me. "She went for a walk upon arriving at the castle, and returned looking quite agitated. When I inquired of her well-being, she said nothing was wrong, though I am certain I have not misjudged her emotional state."

I was going to say that Lieutenant Hammersmith must have upset her, but I didn't think she would want our uncle knowing she went over there from time to time. He might not think it suitable, and I know she would despise any obstacle that might impede her visits. Why she could not bring herself to feel affection for her

Anthony, who is so clearly suited to her — perfect, in fact — is beyond my understanding.

"It's been a long journey for all of us," I said. "I will speak with her later."

Baron Frankenstein put aside his letter and smiled at me. "You have not really looked at the castle since we returned," he noted. "There are some changes that I think you will like." He stood and led me to the right side of the main entrance. When I saw the large room there, the one I had been trying to renovate into a ballroom, I clapped my hands together in utter delight: The work that had been accomplished in our absence was truly amazing.

"Remarkable! Is it not?" Baron Frankenstein said with delight.

"They have been working very hard," Mrs. Flett commented as she joined us with a tray of tea for my uncle and me.

"Oh, it is wonderful! Wonderful!" I cried. The stone had been scrubbed until it sparkled. Velvet drapes, mirrors, and paintings I had never seen before were hung.

"I took the liberty, miss, of hanging the paintings I found in one of the lower rooms," Mrs. Flett said, sounding nervous about how I would react to this initiative on her part. Gazing around, I saw that they were all landscape paintings done in oil paints. They seemed to depict the Orkneys — not only Gairsay but other of the islands with their mystical, ancient stone formations as well.

"They're lovely," I said with sincerity. "Don't you think so, Uncle?"

When he didn't answer, I turned to search for him and saw that he was transfixed by the oil portrait hanging over the heavy mantel of the six-foot fireplace.

"I didn't see this when I first came in here," he said to Mrs. Flett.

"I've just now had the men hang it," she told him. "As you can see, it is very large and quite heavy, so I needed several of the men to lift it."

The portrait showed a tall, handsome man dressed in breeches, boots, a tailed coat, and a ruffed shirt. Thick brown hair was brushed off his angular face and fell nearly to his shoulders. The most striking aspect of the painting was the intense dark eyes that blazed from beneath an intelligent, furrowed brow.

Baron Frankenstein did not speak to me immediately but remained transfixed by the painting, as was I. In truth, he did not have to say a word for me to know the identity of the man, for the resemblance alone was enough to tell me who it was.

"Giselle, meet your father," my uncle said at last. "Meet Victor Frankenstein."

"My father. At last," I murmured, riveted.

Tears misted my eyes as I gazed upon the father who had always been such a mystery, the man who had abandoned two daughters.

He had come for us, at last.

CHAPTER TWENTY-ONE

FROM THE JOURNAL OF
INGRID VDW FRANKENSTEIN

July 1, 1815

After hours of intensive reading, I needed a rest and made my way downstairs. I encountered Giselle as she was coming from her bedroom.

"Have you seen the portrait of our father yet?" she asked. When I told her I hadn't, she grabbed my hand. "Come, quickly. You must see it right away."

I have to tell you, it was a powerful moment for me. There he was — handsome, fiery, proud.

"It made me cry when I first saw it," Giselle admitted. "Uncle

Ernest tells me he looks to be in his twenties — it must have been painted when he resided here."

I nodded but found I didn't have the impulse to weep. I was overwhelmed, just the same. Here was the face of the man whose journals were filling my days and nights. He was suddenly more real to me than he had ever been in my entire life.

"Who could have been stalking him all those years?" I wondered aloud, still gazing up at the dramatic figure in the painting.

"Someone he owed a debt to?" Giselle guessed. We hadn't discussed it much, ever since I had recounted my conversation with our uncle to her.

"Possibly," I agreed. "But what kind of debt could cause a person to hound another in such a way? This person went so far as to murder the ones our father loved. What kind of fiend could be so resolute in his desire for revenge?"

"Or *her* desire," Giselle added.

"I suppose so. Even in this painting, he seems as if he is being pursued," I observed. "I wonder who painted it."

Giselle moved closer to the portrait and stood on tiptoes to read the artist's signature aloud. "John Singleton Copley." Her eyes went wide. "He is a famous American painter, Ingrid. He painted American presidents!"

"Was Victor Frankenstein that famous?" I questioned.

"Perhaps Copley was not yet so well known when he painted this," Giselle suggested.

"Do you think he could tell us anything about our father? He must have known him."

"If the man is still alive, I will invite him to our party," Giselle said. She handed me a sheet of paper on which she'd listed the people she wanted to invite. "Joseph Turner?" I asked. "Another famous painter? Do we dare invite all these celebrated people?"

"Why not?" Giselle challenged.

"Will these people be staying with us?"

"Of course! There are so many rooms in this house that have yet to be opened; we only have to dust them out and revive their furniture. We certainly have the space. Wouldn't it be fun to have the place filled with fascinating people?"

"The chemist Humphry Davy?" I questioned excitedly as I continued to read. Anthony had lent me Davy's book from 1806, *On Some Chemical Agencies of Electricity*, and I was even now reading it. It was utterly fascinating! "Do you think he would come?"

"I read in the paper that he is on an eighteen-month European tour with his assistant and his wife. Why not come to a grand party with notable thinkers?"

"You don't think it a little presumptuous to invite famous people we don't know?"

"Ingrid, we are from a well-known family. I am a baroness, as are you. We live in a castle!"

"Which is looking lovely, by the way," I remarked.

"Yes, isn't it? They've done a remarkable job. We live in a *lovely* castle, which anyone would like to see."

"Do you think Berzelius will come from Stockholm?" I asked hopefully.

From the doorway, someone grumbled, and we both turned toward the sound. It was that arrogant fool, Riff. His gaze ran over us with that same insulting lechery as before.

"Hasn't my uncle dismissed you yet?" Giselle snapped coldly.

"He told my aunt to do it," Riff answered nonchalantly. "Auntie Agnes would never fire her own nephew, though."

"It's not up to her to decide," Giselle insisted. "My sister and I are your employers — and we want you gone! You may collect whatever money is owed to you this Friday when everyone else is paid."

"Don't be a nasty girl," he taunted. "You are much too pretty for that. I only came by to say I found this." He held up a large ornate key. "I thought you might like to have it."

At once I was at his side, eager to get the key from him. He held it away from me, above my head. He was taller than I, and it exceeded my reach.

"Give it to her!" Giselle commanded angrily.

"Do I still have my job?" Riff bargained.

"No!" Giselle told him.

"Then no key," he said.

Giselle colored red with fury. "We'll have you arrested. The police will take that key from you."

"Not if I bury it. I'll deny ever having seen it. Besides, the police on this island are all related to me."

"Let him stay on, Giselle," I pleaded. It looked so much like the key in my dream. I just had to have it, to see.

"Very well," Giselle huffed, turning her back to us.

Riff handed me the key with a grin. "See you around, shoddy science sister."

How I loath the conceited idiot!

Now I had the key. But what was it for? What might it unlock for me? I gazed up at the portrait of Victor Frankenstein, feeling he must know the answer to that question. If only he could speak to me. Gazing at the key nestled in my palm, I had the uncanny idea that maybe he *was* speaking to me.

But what was he saying?

CHAPTER TWENTY-TWO

FROM THE DIARY OF

BARONESS GISELLE FRANKENSTEIN

July 2, 1815

Diary, I cannot tell you how busy I have been, planning this party. I scarcely have time to think! I intend to send out fifty invitations, which is utter madness, but I would like nothing better than for all fifty to answer in the affirmative. What a gala it will be!

The party itself must match or even better the luster of the guest list. Ingrid is aghast at the audacity of my inviting these famous personages of the arts, literature, politics, and philosophy. While in mainland Scotland, I picked up copies of two newspapers, *The Edinburgh Review* and *The Quarterly Review*, from which to cull the names of any person of note mentioned in the paper. To this I will add noted scientific minds from a list Ingrid made for me on the trip back from Edinburgh. Finding their addresses will be a challenge but well worth the effort, I am certain.

It was while I was sitting in the room facing the ocean, perusing *The Quarterly Review* to once more check that I had not overlooked anyone of note, that Baron Frankenstein inquired as to why the infuriating Riff remained on the premises. I told him what had transpired.

"Why was Ingrid so avid to possess that key?" he inquired.

I threw my arms wide in exasperation. "She said she'd dreamed of it."

"Dreamed of it?"

"Yes — saw it in a dream."

"Was it a large, decorative key?"

When I confirmed that it was, he shook his head. "That poor foolish girl! She didn't see the key in a dream. More likely she noticed it hanging on a hook in the walk-in cool room. It opens the root cellar behind it."

"Perhaps she noticed it without realizing, and then dreamed of it," I speculated. "Dreams often work that way."

"I agree, they do," Baron Frankenstein said. "The fellow was toying with you. I will go talk to Mrs. Flett, and, if need be, I will dismiss the young ruffian myself."

"It will be a relief to have him gone," I said. Baron Frankenstein went off to find Mrs. Flett, and I stared out the window at the vivid blue of the sky. We were so far above the ocean that the sky was all that was visible from the first floor, though the crash of waves and calls of seabirds filled the room through the open window. My mind drifted to the first day I had seen Riff, and how flattered I'd felt by his long appreciative gaze, even though I knew it was not a proper way to feel about such unabashed lechery. It was too bad that he'd turned out to be so boorish. I had learned my lesson about boors.

July 3

Today I awoke the moment Ingrid appeared in the doorway, looking feverish with excitement.

"Come with me, Giselle! I think I know what door this key opens."

"I do too," I revealed gently. "Our uncle told me it unlocks a door in the root cellar behind the kitchen pantry."

An expression of unbelieving confusion spread across her face as my words hit her. "It can't be. I was so sure," she objected.

Rising from my bed, I quickly dressed and took her hand in order to lead her toward the kitchen. "Let's see for ourselves," I suggested, thinking it would be better if I were with her to help her with her disappointment. As we went, I told her all that Baron Frankenstein had said to me about how the dreadful Riff had fooled us by implying that the key had more importance than it really did. When we got there, the kitchen was empty, and I lit an oil lantern as Ingrid led me to the door for the pantry.

"Look! Here is the key Uncle Ernest meant!" she cried triumphantly, pointing at a nearly identical key hanging on a nail just outside the door. Taking down the key, I placed it in Ingrid's hand beside the one she'd gotten from Riff. The only difference was a nick chipped into the metal of the key from Riff.

We gazed at each other uncertainly and then cautiously descended the steps into the blackness of the pantry. Holding hands, we tried to stay within the halo of the light from the lantern, which tossed eerie forms on the wall. We shivered as our own shadows formed giant ghostly images.

"Go all the way to the back wall," Ingrid instructed me, her voice tense with excitement.

A small white mouse scurried across my boot, causing me to scream and jump, knocking Ingrid to the side.

"Hold your light up. See where it runs!" she ordered.

Doing as she commanded, my gaze followed the mouse until it disappeared into the ground under a door in front of us. We quickly made our way to it and felt for the lock, which Ingrid immediately attempted to unlock with the key not containing the nick.

Ingrid pushed the door and it creaked open, presenting to us a room of even more impenetrable blackness, colder than the pantry.

Holding the oil lamp high, I saw empty crates that must have once held carrots, potatoes, turnips, and the like. The little mouse that had just startled me appeared once more, appraising us on two legs from the top of a container, his pink nose twitching. In the next moment, he leapt away, disappearing into the wall behind him.

Ingrid sprang away from me and dashed to the far wall, pounding on it.

"Have you gone mad?" I demanded, hurrying to her side. "What are you doing?"

"Listen, Giselle! Listen!" She pounded hard on the wall. "Listen to the echo. The space beyond this wall is hollow. There's no rock or wood behind it."

Ingrid searched the wall with her eyes and hands as I held the lamp high over my head to throw the maximum light. I searched along with her until my eyes caught sight of a thick iron plate just at the edge of the light.

"There!" I said.

Ingrid held both keys into the light, selected the nicked key, and, with trembling hands, inserted it into the lock. She looked at me, her eyes wide and bright with the thrill of possibly entering an unknown space.

"What do you think is behind the door?" she asked.

The images of insects, snakes, bats, and all manner of rodents flooded my mind, along with the even more horrifying images of human skeletons and ghostly apparitions. And a person. I had such a strong sense that there could be someone waiting there. Waiting to hurt us.

"There's only one light," I said, unable to push my irrational thoughts aside. A film of cold sweat was crawling across my skin as my pulse quickened, prompted by the mere idea of being left in this lightless place by myself. I gripped Ingrid's arm. "Please, let's go back. I read once of a castle that had an underground tunnel that was actually a labyrinth. Only the initiated few could find their way through, and everyone else who entered it was instantly confused and perished there in the darkness." I could not imagine any death that could be more horrible than to wander endlessly in a lightless maze.

"Stay here with the lamp and I will be right back."

"You won't be able to see. What good is it if you can't see?"

"I can feel along the walls," Ingrid insisted. "I just want to know how big of a space it is and how far back it goes."

"I can't go with you," I confessed. "I want to, but I can't. I have too much terror of the dark."

"You've already come this far," she pointed out.

It was true, but the way ahead was utterly lacking in even the dimmest glimmer. To me it seemed so deep and fathomless I was sure anything that entered would surely be swallowed up.

"I can't go any farther," I said, choking out the words.

"Can you stay here and hold the light?" Ingrid asked.

"Yes. I think I can," I said with a quivering voice — how I despised myself for being so abject! But there was no choice, my terror was too overpowering. It was something in my blood, in my bones. "Please don't go!"

"I'll be very quick," Ingrid promised. Still in the lamp's glow, she found the wall of the interior room, which appeared to be a long tunnel approximately the width and height of a large grown man.

A grown man.

I watched, trembling, as Ingrid moved down the length of the tunnel, lifting the lantern ever higher to throw a longer circle of light into the empty space. Then, all at once, she was gone.

The flame of the lamp flickered and my heart skipped with panic. And then I heard it. A footstep. It was a man's heavy tread against the stone floor, in tandem with an acrid odor.

"Who's there?" I whispered.

No one answered, but now I could hear breathing. I thought to call for Ingrid, but I did not want to make it known that she was even there.

"Who are you?" I asked again.

A man's hand darted into the light, pulling the lantern from me. I felt the hot oil splatter against my cheek as he dashed it against the wall, plunging us into blackness.

Then the hand gripped me, swinging me against the wall.

CHAPTER TWENTY-THREE

FROM THE JOURNAL OF

INGRID VDW FRANKENSTEIN

July 3, 1815

A most remarkable yet disturbing day. I am overwhelmed with emotion. Frightened . . . yet exhilarated beyond my wildest imaginings. Bold plans whirl in my head. Dread fear enfolds me.

First let me tell you that I have come across a tunnel behind the root cellar. Poor brave Giselle is so troubled by the dark that I had to leave her behind before entering.

I told myself she would be all right there with the lantern. And so I made my way into the tunnel, feeling along the cold stone walls. Slowly my eyes must have dilated to their full potential because I began to discern where the wall and floor met. It's strange to think how much light exists even in the densest blackness. I am thankful for this small measure of vision, otherwise I would surely have plummeted down the wide stairway that opened before me.

It was with a pounding heart that I proceeded onto the spiral steps. I hugged the wall, terrified that I might fall over the outer edge of the steps or slip down them. I seemed to descend for a very long time. After a while, I became disoriented, starting to fear that this was some sort of bottomless stairwell that would never end.

I thought of turning back, but this worsened my condition. Above me I could see nothing, nor anything below. I seemed to hang in a lightless void. All sense of dimension was lost.

For a long while I existed within the most profound stillness I have ever experienced. For the first time ever I realized how accustomed one becomes to the ambient noises all about — the sounds of birds and insects, of the passing air and the rustle of leaves, of all sorts of background hum. But now I was overcome with a terrifying silence. Was I deep underwater? I had to be.

Continuing on in the dark and quiet, I became unnerved. I was thankful to have my hand on the cold, wet wall. It was my only anchor to the tangible world.

After a while I became aware of a pounding, a roaring. Was it machinery? No. I had heard it before, but couldn't place what was causing the sound.

Then it came to me. It was the surf crashing all around.

Oddly, this steady noise helped me to reorient, and mitigated the sensation of floating in nothingness. I was at the bottom of the incline now, and in a new, long tunnel. I inched along as a soft glimmer of light from below began to peel back the darkness. Its glow increased steadily until I could see what was at the end of the tunnel.

At first I could scarcely believe what my eyes were reporting. So unbelievable was the sight before me that I began to suspect I was asleep, dreaming.

The cavernous room at the bottom of the stairs was equipped with scientific materials of every description. Two surgical beds with leather constraints dangling from the sides sat side by side. A long table was jammed with glass beakers, curling tubes, burners, plates, cups, mortar and pestle sets, and other items I couldn't even name. Four large drums were coiled in copper wire that reached all the way up to the towering ceiling, from which the light was fighting its way in.

A gasp of realization shook me.

I knew what I had come upon.

This was my father's laboratory!

Hurrying into the center of it, I examined everything I could find in the dim light. There were surgical scalpels of every description, razor sharp and gleaming. Gauze wrapping and stitching string were in good supply. Labeled jars sat on shelves and in them were specimens of human body organs. Everything was there from a jarred pituitary gland to a full toenail floating in some preserving fluid.

As I surveyed this morbid and sometimes grisly collection with fascination, I came upon a bottom shelf holding three thick, wide albums, much like a portfolio of work an artist might keep. Each was tied closed with string and heavily dust covered. Clearing them caused me to cough and sneeze.

Avidly, I opened the first to an anatomical sketch of sorts. The man it portrayed was pulled apart as though some powerful magnet had yanked his limbs away from one another. Under the drawing, words were scrawled in a handwriting that had become familiar to me over the course of the last weeks. My father's hand.

A body may be assembled as easily as it is disassembled. But what is the animating force?

Alchemy?

Voltage?

Divinity?

Had Victor Frankenstein's great experiment — the one that drove him mad — been the creation of a living human being? What audacity! What vision!

In sketch after sketch, notation upon notation, he detailed how he'd done it. With the help of men like the unsavory Gallagher, he'd assembled all the human parts he needed and had sewn them together like a tailor assembling an elaborate garment of several layers.

He wrote of how it laid there, a lifeless corpse, as experiment after experiment failed to animate it. He soaked his creature in electrolytic metal-infused baths, hoping in vain that it would stir. He wrapped metal wire around its arms and legs and fed current through it until its nails blackened and its hair fried. He was increasingly anguished by it all.

Every night I was oppressed by a slow fever and I became nervous to a most painful degree; the fall of a leaf startled me, and I shunned my fellow-creatures as if I had been guilty of a crime.

My father was conflicted about his creation. He described him as having yellow skin, lustrous black and flowing hair, and teeth of a pearly whiteness. He tells that the creature had *watery eyes, that seemed almost the same color as the dun white sockets in which they were set, his shriveled complexion and black lips.*

But he carried on relentlessly with his efforts to bring the creature to life.

And then at last he struck upon the idea of elevating his creation in the middle of a lightning storm.

All the elements came together that night.

The creature trembled to life.

With a deep intake of breath, I absorbed the impact of what I had just read. My father had brought to life a man of his own creation. Astonishing!

I was confused, though. All his notes indicated that this had taken place at a laboratory in Ingolstadt. What, then, was *this* laboratory?

Gazing upward, I saw the light filtering through a sort of hatchway. The wires from the copper-wrapped drums also extended up through the sides of the hatch. Where did they lead? Were they conductors of electricity?

It was suddenly clear to me. This was an attempt to re-create the laboratory at Ingolstadt. I remembered the tales the Orkneyans told of lights flashing and strange sounds emanating from the castle. Victor Frankenstein had come here six years after his original experiment to . . .

Do what?

Make more people?

A race of new people?

A very high ladder led to the ceiling, and so I began to climb it. At the top, I was able to knock back the hatch with one hand while clinging to the ladder with the other. Sunlight attacked my eyes so fiercely that I turned away as my ears filled with the crash of surf. I made my way onto a simple platform that jutted from the wall. From there I could climb upward.

I emerged into a small one-room cottage. The windows were without glass. Rocks, seaweed, and even small animal skeletons littered the splintered planks of the rough wood on the floor. The thatch of the roof was nearly gone. Pieces of it were strewn on the floor. The copper wires from below extended to the opened roof of this hut, ending in two coils wrapped around an exposed supporting roof beam.

The moment I stepped outside and surveyed my surroundings, I knew exactly where I was. This was the hut on the small stone island out in the sea, the one with the abandoned hovel. Who would ever have imagined that the shed was really the roof of an elaborate and sophisticated underground laboratory?

Tumultuous waves crashed onto the rocks, spraying the bottom of my billowing dress. I yanked loose the ribbons that held my braid to let the wind rip the weave apart until my curls were tangling on the currents of air. Exhilarated as never before in my life, I was transformed. Seventeen years have passed since my father attempted his first experiments. Tremendous strides have been made in science. With his notes and drawings to guide me, I can take his work further than he ever dreamed.

Soon, though, my elation gave way to guilty shame. I had left Giselle awaiting me in the dark tunnel!

And then I spied her, standing up on the edge of the cliff. Her clothing was torn.

I waved to her but she didn't seem to notice me.

"Giselle!" I shouted, waving broadly. The wind carried my voice out to sea.

A warped and rickety rowboat had been pulled ashore by the back of the wrecked hut, its paddles stowed. What luck! It would bring me home without having to find my way back through the frightening tunnel.

It took all my strength to shove the rowboat from the rocks. It bobbed against the sea, threatening to float off with each crash of a passing current. Unable to swim, I hesitated. What if I was thrown back into the swirling sea? It would be the certain end of me. Which was worse, my terror of the ocean or the endless silent tunnel?

Glancing up, I watched the torn strips of Giselle's ripped clothing flapping in the wind. Her disheveled hair whirled around her head.

Taking the rowboat would bring me to her much more quickly than groping blindly through the tunnel.

Steeling my nerves, I threw myself into the rocking boat. I fumbled with the splintered oars and rowed over the chopping waves. Water crashed over the sides, soaking me again and again. It burned my eyes and left the taste of salt on my tongue.

When finally — with immeasurable relief — I made it within a yard of the shore, I slid out onto the craggy bottom and dragged the boat in. Sitting a moment, I wrung out my sodden skirt.

I sat only a moment, knowing I must reach Giselle. I rose but could see no way up the steep cliff.

The clatter of hooves made me turn. Walter was riding toward me.

"Are you all right?" he asked, coming to a halt alongside me.

"Yes! Quite all right!" I said. "But can you tell me how to get up the cliff? I must get to my sister, who is above us and in some distress."

He extended a hand, which I clasped with both of my own. In an instant he'd drawn me up and I sat in front of him in his saddle. Before I could say a word, we were riding through the surf and up a winding path that led back toward the castle. When we reached Giselle, he stayed mounted while guiding me down to the ground.

Giselle ran to me, throwing herself into my arms, sobbing. "You're safe! Thank heavens!"

"What happened, Giselle?" I cried.

"There's something in that tunnel! It attacked me!"

"Did you see it?"

"No!"

"Was it human or animal?"

"I don't know. Human, I think."

"How did you escape?"

"I fought! I fought for my life! It was horrible, Ingrid! I was so scared. But I fought and I got away."

She laid her head on my shoulder and sobbed, her body trembling. Glancing at Walter, I tried to ascertain his reaction to all this.

He didn't even notice me. He was transfixed by Giselle, staring at her as though she were the loveliest woman he had ever seen.

CHAPTER TWENTY-FOUR

FROM THE DIARY OF

BARONESS GISELLE FRANKENSTEIN

July 4, 1815

Ingrid has told me that the tunnel she traveled down comes up at the hovel out on Sweyn Holm, the tiny, rugged island off the shore beneath our castle. I believe her but have no desire to see it for myself, as the idea of the dark and narrowness of a tunnel fills me with terror. She has sworn me to secrecy. She claims she will keep all the inner doors locked so that no one may enter the castle from the island. It will be her own refuge.

But where is my refuge?

I don't want to think about what happened, or write about what happened. I must put it out of my mind, if I am to go on. It was so terrifying that I can't bear to remember it.

"You should not be in that tunnel," I warned her this evening. "Something is there."

"You must not say anything — if you do, everyone will know about the passage. If we must talk to police, say you were attacked in the pantry or the root cellar," she begged.

I don't want scandal surrounding the castle. Nothing must soil this event that I'm working so assiduously to make the social event that all of Europe will be talking about. It will be our introduction to high society and the exciting world of the most fashionable and interesting friends.

I will not jeopardize that.

July 6, 1815

A young man came to the door of the castle this afternoon claiming to be from the Edinburgh constabulary. Baron Frankenstein invited him in and asked Mrs. Flett to serve us some tea in the far room facing the ocean. I found him rather good-looking, of medium build with sandy blond hair.

"I have come to inquire if you know of the whereabouts of one Johann Gottlieb. He seems to have quite disappeared. His father is searching for him and gave us your name as one who might know," he said.

At the sound of Johann's name I grabbed my wrist with the opposite hand to suppress the hard shudder that ran through my body. Johann had disappeared? How could that be?

"You are American?" Ingrid noted, no doubt judging from his speech.

"My mother is a Scot, my father American," he replied. "Do you know Johann Gottlieb?"

"Johann returned home with his father, didn't he, Giselle?" Ingrid said, turning to me.

"I presumed that was his plan," I confirmed, "although it's only an assumption, not anything he actually told me."

"Did he speak of going anywhere else?" Investigator Cairo asked.

"He spoke of wanting to travel all over Europe," I revealed, and then laughed bitterly at the memory. "He was hoping to use my money to fund his travels and so asked me to marry him. I declined."

This caused the investigator to raise a quizzical eyebrow. I told him of my suspicion that Johann was a fortune hunter.

"I see," he said, writing something on a notebook he took from his coat pocket. "Did you two quarrel about this?"

I admitted that we had, though I didn't tell him how Johann had attacked me, since Ingrid and I had agreed not to let Baron

Frankenstein know of this. He was giving us a very free rein, and we did not want him to feel he needed to be overprotective, thus limiting our considerable freedom.

"And Mr. Gottlieb has not contacted you since?" Investigator Cairo asked.

"I did not expect to hear from him after that, and so didn't think it strange when no letter arrived," I said. "Why? You say he has disappeared?"

"Yes. We were hoping you might have some insight into his whereabouts. In fact, his father was hoping that he had actually come here, with you."

"I can assure you, he did not," I said.

"I see that is no doubt true."

He grew pensive and asked questions regarding our staff and then about our neighbor, Lieutenant Hammersmith.

"Why are you asking about him?" Ingrid inquired.

"No reason in particular. I just wanted to know how well you know him."

"He's a distinguished military man, and he is recovering from wounds incurred while fighting Napoleon's troops as well as a nerve disease," Ingrid said. "I am sure he is most reputable, and there is no reason to suspect him."

"I see," the investigator said, and made a note. He turned to our uncle. "Do you have a gun in the house, Baron Frankenstein?"

My uncle said he did not, and Investigator Cairo advised him to get one. "I've talked to the local constables here. It seems there have been some strange things going on in this area of late, so it doesn't hurt to have protection."

A curious gleam in the investigator's eye signaled to me that he knew more things he wasn't telling us. I imagined he had talked to our local police before seeing us, and had heard all the latest gossip. I wasn't going to give him the satisfaction of passing the gossip on further, but Ingrid wasn't as reluctant.

"What sorts of things?" she asked, looking alarmed at what he was telling us.

"Surely locals talk, don't they?" he replied. Then, staring at me, he said, "Or maybe they don't talk to you."

"What have you heard?" Baron Frankenstein asked, also intrigued.

"You must know that a sea captain, a Captain Ramsay, who runs his boat back and forth from Kirkwall to Gairsay was found floating in the bay a couple of weeks ago? It's possible he got tangled in the lines of his sailboat or the mast came around and took him unawares, but some people believe he was strangled."

"Strangled!?" Ingrid cried.

Investigator Cairo nodded solemnly as he consulted his notepad. I waited for Ingrid or my uncle to mention that I had been with him just before he died, but neither did. Since I did not like the investigator's demeanor, I did not volunteer this information either.

Cairo continued, "Do you know an Arthur Flett? I have been told he is employed here."

"Many men named Flett work here," I said. "They are a large family on the island. I don't know all of their first names."

"I will ask Mrs. Flett," Baron Frankenstein offered. He got up and left the room.

"Why are you inquiring about Arthur Flett?" Ingrid asked, sitting forward in her chair.

"His family says he has been missing for almost two days, and he was last seen here."

Ingrid and I looked at each other, puzzled, as Baron Frankenstein returned. "Arthur Flett is that fellow called Riff," he announced. "I had him dismissed last Monday," he added, turning to the detective. "I didn't care for his presumptuous manner."

"How did he react to being fired?" Investigator Cairo asked.

"He was not pleased, naturally."

I said, "He attempted to have us intervene on his behalf, and I agreed, just to be rid of him. But I didn't say anything to my uncle." A quick glance of understanding ran between Ingrid and me, reinforcing a tacit agreement not to speak of the key involved, since I had promised not to reveal the tunnel. Perhaps it was not as discreet as we'd hoped because Investigator Cairo paused to scribble a note in his book.

"I imagine that he's gone off somewhere to spend the last of his pay, cheering himself up in the taverns over in Kirkwall," Baron Frankenstein proposed. "His aunt tells me he is quite the ladies' man. I'd wager he'll come staggering back onto the island sometime when he's good and ready."

Investigator Cairo stood, indicating that he was finished questioning us, and handed a card to Baron Frankenstein. "Thank you for your time. Please be in touch with me at this address over in Kirkwall. It's where I'll be staying until we get to the bottom of this. I am helping the local constables with their investigations while I am here."

"Certainly," our uncle agreed.

"Ladies, good day." With a nod to Ingrid and me, Investigator Cairo left, escorted to the door by Baron Frankenstein.

As soon as they were gone from the room, Ingrid gripped my arm. "What do you think of all this?"

I didn't know what to think, but it was surely frightening and upsetting. "The captain must have gotten tangled in his lines. Awful as he was, I never should have left him there," I said.

"You couldn't have known he was tangled," Ingrid assured me.

Our uncle returned, scowling fretfully, and sat heavily in a chair. "I was going to tell you girls that I would be leaving soon, now that you are settled, but I think perhaps I should stay for a while longer."

"Should we have told him I was with Captain Ramsay? It may have been shortly before he died."

"Why involve yourself with the police?" Baron Frankenstein replied.

I suddenly felt very guilty about not divulging this piece of information, and knew it would bother me if I didn't say something. I hurried to the door, bolting out to run after the investigator as he made his way down the hill.

"Investigator!" I shouted. He turned, waiting for me to reach him.

I told him how the boat had capsized because I stood up and that I felt badly now that I hadn't stayed to see if he was all right. "It's understandable," he said. "You had no obligation to stay. The water was not deep. Besides, someone might have come along later, while he was struggling with the sailing lines, and strangled him. If indeed there was any strangulation. It was best that you weren't still there."

"Do you think some dangerous person has come to the island?" I asked.

"It's possible," he allowed. "You should be careful."

"That isn't why you're really here, is it?"

He looked at me curiously. "What do you mean?"

"I mean — you say Johann has disappeared. Do you think he may have come here? As some kind of . . . revenge?"

"That is not why I'm here. But certainly, if you see him, you should alert me immediately."

There was something strange about him as he said this. Was there more that he wasn't telling me? A chill suddenly ran up my back as a frightening idea appeared. Before I could stop myself, I asked, "How do I know that *you* are not the dangerous person who has come to the island? How do I know Johann hasn't sent you? I only have your word that he's disappeared."

He dug in the pocket of his coat and showed me some official papers, but they meant nothing to me. "I am from the police. Are you always so suspicious of people?" he asked.

"One can never tell," I replied, backing away from him.

"Do as I say and be careful," he repeated. "For your own safety, don't wander around by yourself."

With a nod, I turned and hurried back to the castle.

Baron Frankenstein was waiting outside the front door. "There you are!" he cried when he saw me. "Why did you run off like that?" he asked with an anger obviously born of worry. I told him I had wanted to tell Investigator Cairo what I knew of Captain Ramsay.

"Don't go off like that anymore," he scolded, and then sighed deeply. "I don't like this one bit. I'm afraid it's all starting again."

"What is?" I asked.

"All of it: the mysterious deaths, the missing persons, the feeling of being stalked by some malevolent force. I will go to Edinburgh tomorrow to purchase a weapon."

"No, please don't leave," I urged him, suddenly frightened. "Lieutenant Hammersmith was in the military; perhaps he has a gun he could loan you."

"Mmm," my uncle murmured, sounding unconvinced. "Perhaps. I wonder if we can trust him, though."

This idea was alarming, since Ingrid was spending so much time with the man. But it was true; we did not know one other person who could verify that he was who he said he was.

I suddenly looked at Baron Frankenstein and realized that the same was true of him. It occurred to me that he didn't look at all like the man in the portrait over the fireplace — if that was, indeed, my father, Victor Frankenstein. How could I be sure that was even really a picture of him?

Stop! I commanded myself. *You're exhausted and scared, so control your imagination.*

Just the same, I am going to bed tonight feeling frightened and out of sorts. I do not like this turn of events one bit.

CHAPTER TWENTY-FIVE

FROM THE JOURNAL OF
INGRID VDW FRANKENSTEIN

July 13, 1815

Late this afternoon, I ran into the investigator who had come to the castle last week. I was down at the harbor waiting for the mail boat to come. At least that was my stated objective. In truth, I was hoping Walter would come down to take out his sailboat and I could meet him "accidentally." In the last week, when I went over to his house, he did not answer the door.

This sudden and unexpected rejection of my company was driving me to distraction. I have no idea what has prompted it. But I have a suspicion too terrible to bear. Indeed my stomach clenches whenever the idea snakes its way into my mind. Was he dismissing me because he had become enamored of Giselle?

Oh, I cannot — even now — stand to write such a thing. I longed to ask him and hear him say, "Not at all. You silly thing! How could you think it?" It would be all I needed. But without seeing him to get this reassurance, I feel I'm going mad.

"Hello there," Investigator Cairo greeted me as I paced the dock with a feigned nonchalance that was probably none too convincing.

"Are you heading back to the mainland?" I asked, just to be cordial.

"I am. And you, Baroness Frankenstein? What brings you here?"

"The mail boat."

"You seem agitated. Are you waiting for an important letter?"

Once more, he was at the edge of impudence. "I seem agitated?" I questioned skeptically. So much for my attempt to seem casual.

This made him chuckle. "As I said earlier, you must excuse me. I am an investigator and a student of human behavior. I have read the works of Joseph Guillotin on the nerves and of Descartes. Currently I am reading about François Magendie, known for his vivisection of the nerves. I have attended lectures in London given by Dr. William Lawrence on the animating force of life. He believes that the body is a mechanism that can be animated by some outside force akin to electricity — maybe even electricity itself."

As you might imagine, he had my full and enthusiastic attention.

"This is unbelievable! I have just finished studying with Count Volta in Italy," I told him excitedly.

"He was experimenting with muscle stimulation through electric shock," Investigator Cairo exclaimed. "I know his work well. And this interests you?"

"It interests me very much. You can't imagine how much. I would even say it is a passion with me."

"For me the passion is to understand the inner workings of the mind as they manifest in behavior," he said ardently. "Being able to read people accurately is invaluable. Any method that might shed light on the inner essence of a human being is crucial beyond words."

"Can you read me?" I asked.

"I've already told you . . . you're agitated. And you're in love."

The instant burn on my checks told me I was blushing. I turned away. How uncanny!

Again he chuckled. "That's all right. Don't be embarrassed. To be in love is to be agitated. Are you really awaiting the mail? Do you await a letter from your beloved? Or is the object of your affection coming into the harbor?"

"He might be coming to the harbor," I admitted, surprised by my own candor. "I was hoping I might run into him."

"And instead it is only I, the investigator, who comes along. Sorry."

Now it was my turn to laugh. "That's fine. Really. I have enjoyed our conversation." The ferry to Mainland came into view and Investigator Cairo backed slowly toward it. Then he stopped as an idea struck him.

"You know who you should find out about?" he said.

"Who?"

"A fellow named Jean-Baptiste Sarlandière. He was in the French military when I met him a few years ago, but we have kept up a correspondence. He has recently returned to his medical work. He writes me that he is starting to experiment with what he calls electropuncture. He's using acupuncture needles from China on the surface of the skin to conduct electricity across the body. He claims this has great restorative effects. Despite his youth, Sarlandière's work is brilliant."

The ferry horn indicated that he had to board. With a wave to me, he ran off to claim his seat.

Even though the mail boat did not bring me any mail, and

Walter did not appear, it appears my journey to the dock was not an entirely fruitless one.

July 14, 1815

I have seen Walter today, at last. And what an encounter it was!

It was an unusually hot day. The constant wind had disappeared and all was strangely still. Donning my lightest summer dress, I headed once more to Walter's cottage, determined not to be shut out. If I had to throw a rock and shatter his window in order to crawl through, I was prepared to do it.

When I arrived, though, he was outside behind his cottage. He sat in a wooden outdoor chair, the pant leg of his missing leg pinned up. "Ingrid," he greeted me with enthusiasm, as if there had been no estrangement between us. He even honored me with one of his rare, if quick, smiles.

"Where have you been, Walter?" I asked as I approached him. "Why have you been avoiding me?"

"Not at all. I've been busy and —"

"Walter!" I cried. "Don't! Tell me the truth. I've been so worried."

Facing me, his eyes darted as though a million thoughts were sparking all at once in his mind.

"I'm glad to see you, Ingrid," he said at last.

Foolish me! I nearly cried with happiness at those words.

At the same time, I wanted to fling myself at him and pound his chest with angry fists. Was that all he could say after all these days of anguish he'd caused me?

"I'm happy to see you too, Walter," I said, coming very close to him. "But why have you shut me out?"

He struggled up and perched on the side arm of the chair. At this angle we were nearly eye to eye. With a sudden sweeping movement that snatched away my breath, he grabbed me around the waist with his left arm and kissed me.

Crippled though he was, he was also astoundingly strong.

My stunned surprise melted quickly to passion.

I threw my arms around his neck, returning his ardor.

We kissed and kissed . . . and kissed. I was lost in a world of kisses. A world of Walter. His scent, his breath, his touch. There was no other reality but Walter. Kissing me at last.

Walter took my arm and sank down into the chair, drawing me into his lap. There he kissed me passionately once more. After some time of this we stopped, and sat gazing into each other's eyes.

"I love you, Ingrid," he said quietly.

How my heart leapt with joy! But I was confused.

"If you feel like this, Walter, then why have you shunned my company?" I asked.

"Because I love you and I know my love is selfish," he replied.

"I love you too," I said breathlessly. "So how can your sweet love be selfish?"

"I am a shell, a wreck, Ingrid. To ask for your hand is the most hideous kind of selfishness. It would be wrong. I have nothing to offer you."

How my heart went to him. Such anguish! "You have yourself to give, Walter. It's all I want."

"It's not enough. You would be my nursemaid."

"I wouldn't mind."

"Not at first, but eventually you would."

"And it's not because you have fallen in love with Giselle?" I had to know.

He pulled back to scrutinize me with disbelief. "Your agitated sister?"

"Don't you think her beautiful?"

"Yes, I do. Incredibly beautiful."

My heart sank.

"But the two of you are identical," Walter added.

"She is the radiant, attractive one. I am a duck to her swan."

At this, Walter threw his head back, erupting with laughter. It was the first time I had ever heard this wonderful sound. "*You* are the one who radiates intelligence and warmth. You are her equal in beauty, but it is your inner being that makes you so precious to me."

"I am precious to you?" I asked softly, just to hear him affirm it.

He pulled me even closer. "So precious, you can't imagine."

"And you no longer think your love is selfish?" I asked hopefully.

He smiled sadly. "Not at all. I know it is selfish of me."

"Then what has changed?"

"I have given in to the truth."

"What is that?" I asked.

"I am a selfish man."

Pressing against him, I held him tight, saying nothing more. I was too filled with happiness to speak.

"Things must stay as they are," he warned me. "Know that I love you, but there can be no life together. It's not right."

I rested my head on his shoulder. It was blissful to be so close. "Knowing you love me is enough for now," I said honestly.

Turning, he kissed my cheek and let his head rest against mine. We sat there in loving togetherness until he drifted off to sleep. Disentangling slowly, I left him there to nap.

Oh, Walter! My Walter! I thank the heavens for your "selfishness." You love me! This night I am the happiest young woman alive!

July 20, 1815

I have been spending countless hours down in the laboratory reading the new set of albums I found down here, almost without pause. No one could blame me for the breathless fascination I bring to this endeavor. The information contained in these large volumes is beyond belief.

Victor Frankenstein succeeded in creating a real human being . . . and in these albums, he tells exactly how he did it. Exactly! Every step is recorded in minute detail.

All his feelings of triumph are summed up in one hastily penned, exalted scrawl: *IT'S ALIVE!!!!*

I still have not discovered what brought him here nearly six years later. I can only assume it was to continue his work. I will keep reading in search of this answer.

There is another reason beyond fascination and curiosity why I need to master the information here. Things are not going well for Walter. These past several days his condition has worsened and he hardly gets out of bed. He is in tremendous pain. How my heart aches to see him so. I have asked Mrs. Flett for various herbal remedies I have seen her dispense to the workmen. Walter tries them but they help only a little.

Walter says he has a doctor on the mainland of Scotland. He plans to go see him soon. I don't see how he can accomplish this if his condition does not improve.

I am convinced that these albums hold the key to grafting new body parts to him. If my father could build an entire human, would it not be possible to graft on a new leg or replace a withered hand? New tree limbs from other varieties are connected to existing trees. If Victor Frankenstein could reawaken dead nerve endings with a bolt of lightning, why not bring them to life with the more controllable buzz of a voltaic battery?

In one of Anthony's volumes, I have found reference to the ancient Asian practice of acupuncture. I keep thinking of Sarlandière's work, which Investigator Cairo told me about — combining acupuncture with electricity. Electropuncture. I am resolved to write Anthony to see if he can find a set of acupuncture needles for me.

My father's legacy must continue.

CHAPTER TWENTY-SIX

FROM THE DIARY OF

BARONESS GISELLE FRANKENSTEIN

July 20, 1815

Dear Diary, these days I am haunting the harbor, awaiting all the supplies I have ordered: linen napkins, tablecloths, china, glasses, silverware. And the food must be exquisite, so I have commissioned multiple food shipments: quail eggs; caviar from Normandy and cheeses from Paris; Champagne; scones from Aberdeen; jams and jellies from Glasgow; smoked herring from Amsterdam to complement our own local oysters. Oh, the list is endless. It's so nice to have such a supply of money!

When the mail boat arrived, the captain handed me a bundle of letters tied together, and it was all I could do to keep from ripping them open there and then, since I could see that they were responses to my invitations. There were no further packages, so I headed back up the dock.

I saw one of the men who deliver food in the morning sitting in his wagon. "Deliver your packages for you?" he offered, and I knew this meant he would do it for a fee and not out of friendliness.

"No packages today, thank you," I declined, hardly looking up from the bundle of envelopes I was perusing.

"Give you a ride?" he asked.

"No, thank you." It was a lovely day and I preferred to walk.

The man grumbled under his breath, and I turned to look at him. It sounded like "Damn foreigner," though I still get confused by the heavy Orkneyan dialect.

"Excuse me?" I challenged him. "Did you say something?"

"Too good to take a ride in my wagon?" he sneered.

That he said clearly enough, making sure I would understand.

I felt like telling him that maybe I *was* too good for it, especially if he was going to be so hostile. I forbore, though, and instead ignored him.

I was halfway up the winding road to the castle when I could stand the suspense no longer and settled on one of the stone walls bouldering the side of the road. It was a quiet spot, and I thought it a good place to sit and cut open my party responses using the steel letter opener I'd brought in my skirt pocket for just such a purpose. I was busy splitting open envelopes and sorting them into piles of *yes* and *no* when the same carriage driver pulled up alongside me.

He came upon me so quietly that I startled and fell forward, slipping from my rock perch to my knees. Looking up from where I'd fallen, I saw the man standing over me, reaching down for me.

I had the strong sensation that I didn't want to touch his hands, so I scrambled to my feet on my own. Not wanting to hear any more of his nastiness, I hurried away.

After about ten minutes, Uncle Ernest came up the road behind me. "I'm so glad to see you, Uncle," I said. "A man nearly ran me off the road with his wagon. Did you see him?"

"No. Did you recognize him?"

"I think he delivers milk and cheese to Mrs. Flett in the mornings."

"Are you all right?" he inquired.

"I fell down."

"You've scraped yourself," he said, observing the blood on my hands. "You must have done it when you fell."

I noticed that there was blood splattered on my envelopes too. I had clutched them too quickly after I'd picked myself up. When I tried to rub the blood off, it only smeared.

I don't know why I'm even bothering to tell you all this, Diary. It's just that I wonder why some of the men on this island are so rough and unpleasant. I am very happy that people of a more refined, educated caliber will be arriving here soon. Perhaps there is a way to convince them to stay and build homes here so that we could have neighbors who aren't as desolate as the ones we do have.

CHAPTER TWENTY-SEVEN

FROM THE JOURNAL OF

INGRID VDW FRANKENSTEIN

July 23, 1815

Good news! Walter has improved greatly. When I went to see him yesterday he was up and sitting. "Do you think Mrs. Flett's remedies have helped?" I inquired, taking his hand as I sat beside him.

He shook his head. "Not really. My illness has its cycles and this last one has run its course. I'll be much improved until it flares again."

"Maybe it won't flare again," I suggested hopefully.

Drawing me to him, he kissed my lips. My eyes shut as I floated in the utter bliss of his touch.

"Maybe it won't flare again," he said softly. But I could tell from his glum, wistful tone that the statement was more a hopeful dream than something he really believed possible.

"Ingrid, I am going away for a short while. I don't want you to worry. I feel well enough for a trip to see my doctor. His office is in Inverness. It's not very far."

"Shall I go with you?" I offered.

"No. It is more restful for me not to keep up conversation. And this treatment will require me to be away from you. I would worry."

I leaned my head against his arm. "All right. I'll miss you."

"And I you."

"Will this treatment help you greatly?" I asked.

"I doubt it."

At that moment it dawned on me that, in the back of my mind, I've been harboring the hope that the power of my love might be enough to cure him. And, in a way, it could be possible. My love can cure him. But not without effort, as I've been hoping. The mere fact that I love Walter with all my heart and soul will not be enough. It's time to kick my lazy mind into action. I'm the daughter of a scientific genius. It's time I began acting as such.

August 3

Yesterday I fell asleep down in the laboratory. For the last ten days I have almost lived down here, searching my father's writings for the key to helping Walter. Giselle and Uncle Ernest worry about me so I appear at the castle only long enough to eat and assure them I am still alive. I want to use this time while Walter is away to the best advantage.

Hopefully he is all right and benefitting from his doctor's treatment. He had so little faith in the outcome, though. I have become obsessed with his cure.

Where do I start? Do I replace his injured parts? Do I run current through his body to recharge his nerves? Would this be a permanent fix or a temporary remedy that needed constant repetition? And if it required repeating, would his body be able to withstand it? Could he withstand the treatments even once?

How I anguish over these things! I pull at my hair as I read volume after volume searching for the key. The key! I relive my dream where Anthony tells me I need the key.

Dr. Sarlandière has not yet replied to the party invitation I had Giselle send. How I pray he comes! More and more I suspect that his work is relevant to my cause.

August 10

Walter has not returned. After ten days I went to check on him. The woman who cares for him was there cleaning and tending the horse. She complained that she had not heard from him or been paid. I gave her what money I had in my bag and asked that she let me know the minute she hears from him.

I have been working tirelessly, reading and taking notes until my eyes burn. I try not to worry about Walter, but it isn't easy.

Today I fell asleep in a chair down in the lab with another of my father's albums still opened on my lap. When I awoke, I saw that the light was not quite so dazzling as it had been earlier. This did not tell me exactly how late it was, only that it was sometime in the evening. It is unsettling to live in a place where darkness never comes and the restorative quiet of the night is lost.

Longing for fresh air, I climbed the tall ladder up into the hovel and stepped out onto the rocky, windswept island. Immediately I was alert to the white sails of a boat out on the ocean. There is a distinctive pendant on the top of the vessel that I recognized as Walter's — he has returned!

How my heart exploded with relief and happiness! But why hadn't he sent word that he was home?

I made my way to the edge of rock overlooking the ocean. There I sat and watched him for a while. He kept coming nearer and his horse was on the beach so I assumed he might be coming in.

Restless, I began to wander the island. Random thoughts floated through my head as I listened to the call of the seabirds, the crash of the surf, and the roar of the wind.

Is it possible that my father's malevolent nemesis had returned? Are Giselle and I in peril? If he is indeed back, can he be stopped? Reasoned with? Is this nemesis such a fiend that he still seeks vengeance even though my father is now dead?

It was while walking along lost in thoughts of this kind that my eyes fell upon what I at first took to be a large, smooth, moss-covered stone. Or was it a very big bird's egg covered in seaweed? I wasn't sure what a puffin's egg looked like, though the birds were very common on these craggy cliffs.

It bobbed there, hitting the rocky edge of the island as the waves bounced it again and again against the stones. Curious, I squatted by the water and reached for it with my two hands.

No sooner did I have it in my grip than I screeched in horror at its slimy texture and hurled it inland onto the stones. It hit with a sickening plop before turning over once.

I couldn't bear to look at it. Desperate to erase the sensation of slippery softness from my palms, I scrubbed them against my skirt. My fingers had sunk right into its top layer into something nauseatingly gelatinous below.

Slowly, though, curiosity got the better of me and I turned toward it.

At first I couldn't comprehend what I was seeing, but within seconds I made sense of the distorted thing lying there.

It was a human head! Waterlogged! Wrapped in long black hair! Its eyes were milky white, but its features were recognizable.

Screaming with terror, I realized it was Giselle's head!

I screamed. Screamed and screamed at the awful sight. I howled with horror until the rock under me seemed to spin and the blue of the sky was mixed with the brown-black of the rocks in a swirling vortex.

When I awoke from my faint, Walter was sitting beside me. The bow of his boat had been pulled up on the rocks. My head rested on his knee and he held my wrist, his thumb pressed on my pulse.

"Walter!" I cried, disoriented and surprised to see him.

"I saw you collapse. I came to see if you were all right."

The horrid image of the head rushed back, causing me to tremble. "Did you see it, Walter?" I shouted as hysteria began to climb within me once more. "Giselle is dead!"

"No! No!" he said soothingly, holding me tight while I buried my face in his shoulder. "It can't be Giselle. When did you last see her?"

"This morning."

"That head has been in the water a long time."

"Are you sure?"

"Positive. I've seen dead soldiers retrieved from the water. I know what they look like in varying stages of decay. That head

might have been in a case or a bag originally, which would pre-
serve it a while longer than if the fish were nibbling at it."

That made sense. Though even despite its half-rotted state, the
grotesque visage bore a striking resemblance to Giselle. And to
me. It was as if gazing upon my own dead self staring luridly back
at me from the grave.

Horrible! Horrible . . .

"Who could it be?" I wondered.

"I don't know." Walter rocked me softly for a few more minutes
with his good left arm as I clutched his shirt. In a while, I was sufficiently composed to notice that he had acquired a wooden lower
leg. It was the kind one saw in drawings of pirates.

He noticed me gazing at it, aghast. "It's a beauty, isn't it?" he
commented. Though his tone was light, he didn't smile.

"*This* was the treatment you underwent?" I asked.

He nodded.

"Does it help you walk?" I asked.

"It does. Though my knee aches fiercely and I still need a cane."

"What should we do with the head?" I asked.

He held up a white cotton bag about the size of a pillowcase with
a drawstring at one end. "I took this from my boat supply kit."

I cringed at the idea of touching it again. "I couldn't."

"I'll do it." With great difficulty, he got to his feet and hobbled
over to the head. He used his cane to work it into the bag and then

drew the cord shut. "Who would throw a dismembered body into the ocean?" he wondered. "Someone might have been trying to cover up the trail of a murder."

"If I showed you something, do you swear you won't talk to anyone about it?"

"Who would I talk to? I hardly speak to anyone but you anyway."

"Swear?"

"I would raise my right hand, but I can't. Yes, I swear."

Now that I was calmer, I noticed that something about the tone of his voice had changed. His words sounded as though they were somehow impeded, stifled. In the sunlight I could see what looked like a stiffening of the skin that ran up the right side of his face from jaw to cheekbone. Too concerned to be shy, I ran my hand along his cheek. "What's happened there?"

He gazed out to the ocean a moment. "Just another of the joys brought on by my illness."

"Does it hurt?"

"A little," he admitted. "It's difficult to move my jaw and my tongue. Never mind about it. What is it I just swore not to tell?"

"Come with me. I'll show you."

He slowly followed me to the shed and left the sack by the door. He was amazed when I showed him the hatch leading down to the laboratory.

He was even more thunderstruck when I explained what was down there.

"I've heard rumors about Castle Frankenstein," he said when I was through. "It was what I was alluding to the first time we met. I never dreamed there could be a fully equipped scientific laboratory down there."

"It's true. There is."

He shook his head in disbelief.

"Can you manage to descend that ladder?" I asked.

"I think I could get down, though getting back up will be more difficult."

"That's all right. There's another way out, if you don't mind tunnels."

"I'm all right with tunnels," Walter assured me. "I'd better go first. If I fall, I don't want to knock you off the ladder."

"Don't fall, it will only make my task harder," I told him.

"Your task?" he questioned.

I nodded. "You'll see."

It took a long time for Walter to make it down the ladder. Several times I was sure he was about to slip. But I saw that he'd been strong when he was well, and his left arm and hand could still grip remarkably well. When he was halfway down the ladder, I followed.

At the bottom, I showed him everything — the equipment, the body parts in jars, my father's albums. "I can make you better,

Walter," I said as he scanned Victor Frankenstein's notes. "Remember the doctor who thought he could cure you with electric current?" I flipped forward in the album to where my father had written of his contact with Jakob Berzelius, the Swedish chemist. Both of them were sure it could be done. "They figured out how to do it, but couldn't control the electricity. But I think I know how to do that. I could give you a new leg and hand too — parts that will work like they should. I could even put new skin on your face."

"You could, could you?" He was teasing, but only by half. There was an expression of keen interest on his face. "Where would you get these human body parts?"

"I know a man in Edinburgh I could contact."

"You do?" He regarded me with a mixture of incredulity, amusement, and respect. "Aren't you a remarkable girl?" he said appreciatively. "Full of surprises."

"I am." I saw no point in responding with false modesty. I was prepared for this. I understood the concepts involved, and my father had left behind a step-by-step guide to connecting and reconnecting body parts, then animating them.

"Would it be very painful?" Walter asked, which told me he was giving it serious consideration.

"We'll numb you with strong alcohol."

"How long will it take?"

"I don't know," I admitted. "I'll set up a recovery room for you down here. I'll take good care of you."

Walter grew quite pensive, surveying the surroundings, glancing at the albums, looking at me. "Ingrid, do you know why I took my sailboat out today?"

"No."

"I was going to capsize it and drown."

I gasped at the awfulness of this. "No! You couldn't!" My eyes teared at the very thought.

"I was about to do it when I saw you in distress."

Flinging my arms around him, I pressed my cheek against his chest. "Promise me you'll never do anything like that again!"

"I can't promise you that, Ingrid. I don't want to be a sick, sad invalid slowly withering away until there's nothing I can do for myself. Dismal as that sounds, it's the future that lies ahead of me. The physician who amputated my leg said I should prepare for further disintegration."

"No, that can't be!" I said passionately. "I won't allow that to happen."

"I haven't told you the worst of it. This hardening of the flesh on my face will spread. Before too long I will be encased in a mask of hard tissue, unable to speak or swallow. If I manage to survive that, it will continue on until I am in a head-to-toe cast of hardened skin. I will desperately long to die. But by then I'll have lost the ability to end my own life."

Everything within me cried out against this. It couldn't be! It wasn't fair! There had to be a way to change his terrible fate.

"I'm not afraid to die," Walter went on. "But I'm terrified of living in this way. So I have nothing to lose. I say we attempt your experiment. If I die trying, I'll be no worse off than if I'd tossed myself into the ocean today."

"Oh, it will work, Walter." In that moment, I was sure of it. "I will contact my friend Anthony and have him get in touch with the body parts man, Gallagher, for me. As soon as I get the parts from Gallagher, we can start. You'll see! I can do this."

I hugged him tightly as tears overtook me. He let me cry a moment, stroking my hair tenderly. "No more crying now," he said after a while. "You're going to fix my problems, aren't you? Didn't you just tell me that?"

"Yes. I am," I declared, wiping my eyes.

"Then there's no reason to cry, is there?"

"No. You're right," I agreed, filled with new resolve.

Walter gazed up the ladder and shook his head. "I can't climb that. You said there is a tunnel out of here?"

"Yes, I'll light a lamp and we'll go slowly. But first, let me retrieve what we found." I climbed the ladder, took the bag with the head, and then, upon returning to the laboratory, took the head out using a pair of wooden tongs. Then I placed it in a large glass jar from one of the shelves and added some of the preserving fluid that all the other parts were sitting in. I turned the glass around, unable to gaze upon the too-familiar face any longer than necessary.

We went very slowly because of the darkness and Walter's infirmity. But the lamp I'd found down in the laboratory threw a strong light, and so the path was clearer than I remembered it. I had not been back since my first journey to the laboratory, having used the aboveground path for all of my visits since that time.

"Be careful on the steps," I warned, recalling the treacherously steep staircase I'd encountered.

We came up the stairs and headed into the tunnel. Walter held my hand as we crept along with me in the lead. Before we had gone very far, I startled beside Walter, alarmed.

"There's someone in the tunnel," I whispered sharply.

He held my arm protectively. Ahead of us, the dark form of a person sat slumped, blocking our path. In the deep silence of the dark passage, it emitted no sound of breathing. Nor did it move at all.

This silence emboldened us to creep forward cautiously. As we neared, I detected the rank odor of decaying flesh. When we were close enough, I lifted the lantern and gasped. The person in front of us stared up blankly, covered in blood with a large triangular shard of glass plunged into his belly. He was clearly no longer alive.

"I know him," I told Walter.

It was Riff.

My head swam with the possibilities. Had he been killed elsewhere? Did someone kill him here in the tunnel? Was that person still in the tunnel? Had my father's nemesis come back? Was he still lurking in the tunnel?

And then an equally frightening possibility came to me: Was Riff the one who had frightened Giselle here in the dark passageway? Had she accidentally killed him in the course of defending herself?

Even though it was self-defense, I couldn't let her go on trial for murder. She wasn't strong enough.

"Would you hold this?" I asked, handing Walter the oil lamp, which he took from me.

Bending, I grasped Riff's ankles and began pulling him back toward the laboratory.

"Where are you going?" Walter asked.

"Wait for me here," I requested without stopping. "I'll be back soon."

"What are you going to do?"

"I'm taking him to the laboratory. We might not have to get in touch with Mr. Gallagher after all."

CHAPTER TWENTY-EIGHT

FROM THE DIARY OF

BARONESS GISELLE FRANKENSTEIN

August 10, 1815

Diary, I had a most perplexing and disturbing conversation with Ingrid this evening on the subject of Mrs. Flett's nephew, Riff. She asked me if I was certain I hadn't seen him after the day he taunted us with the key. When I told her I hadn't, she continued probing, suggesting that I might have forgotten something, or that there might be some fact I didn't want to reveal. Then she dropped that line of inquiry to ask about the day I was attacked in the tunnel. She wanted to know if I'd seen my attacker, and I assured her that he'd come upon me from behind and that I'd fled without looking back.

Finally I was fed up with all these questions and blew up at her. "What are you trying to say, Ingrid?" I demanded.

Ingrid opened her mouth and then shut it again as though deciding not to continue with her line of thought.

"I just think it odd that he disappeared like that," she said, and I felt there was something insincere in her expression and tone.

I don't like this idea that Ingrid might be keeping something from me. Since girlhood we have never kept secrets from each other, and I don't see why she should start now.

I shall go to bed tonight feeling lonely and desolate, because my best friend in the world is not taking me into her confidence.

August 14, 1815

Party plans are advancing wonderfully well, and I now have a list of thirty definite guests, ten possible, and only ten refusals.

You will not believe the guest list, Diary! It includes Lord Byron; the poet Percy Shelley and his wife, Mary. The artist who painted my father's portrait, John Singleton Copley, has accepted, which is thrilling.

Ingrid will be thrilled to know that all her scholars have accepted. Humphry Davy will be coming with his wife and his assistant, Michael Faraday. A French scholar named Sarlandière accepted immediately, although he was the last to be invited; I suppose the French do love a soirée. I wonder if scholars in general are really the best people to have at a party — who really understands what they're talking about? — but there are enough of them that they can talk amongst themselves. I'm sure Ingrid will keep them all busy with her endless scientific curiosity.

The next crucial thing for me to decide is what I will wear to the party, which really amounts to a debutante ball for Ingrid and me, since it is our introduction to fascinating society. Mrs. Flett has told me that there is a wonderful dressmaker over in Stromness, which is a city on Mainland, the second largest after Kirkwall.

Naturally I wanted Ingrid to make the trip to Stromness along with me; she will certainly need a dress too, but she was busy, as is usual these days. I never see her anymore because the first thing in the morning she rows out to Sweyn Holm, where she holes up in that shed and claims to be studying Anthony's medical books and our father's notes. One might think she was preparing for some important test, the way she has taken to devoting herself completely to her studies. I don't think she even goes over to see Lieutenant Hammersmith anymore, though perhaps that's because he isn't home. I never see his chimney emitting smoke these days.

At any rate, I will take the ferry over to Mainland soon and I will get a suitable dress and probably have to buy one for Ingrid as well, or she is likely to show up at the party in her plain frock with an apron thrown over it, her hair in a braid.

The dressmaker in Stromness proved to be a treasure, and I have commissioned her to create a gown with a black velvet top and a plaid taffeta skirt. For Ingrid, I requested that she create a simple dress all in an exquisite sapphire blue silk, which I think suits her style perfectly. My measurements sufficed for the two of us, of course, though I will have to insist that she make the trip back with me when the time comes to pick up the dresses so that she can have one real fitting.

On the ferry back, I ran into Investigator Cairo, who was making another trip to Gairsay from Kirkwall. He waved when he saw me and gave a friendly nod as he came to my side.

"It's a bit late for you to be traveling unescorted, isn't it, Baroness Frankenstein?" he remarked as we stood near the railing.

"Perhaps. But in a place with no darkness, where is the danger?" I replied.

"You make a good point, but enjoy it while you can. Come the winter months, it will be almost nothing but darkness, with only a few hours of dim sunlight."

"I won't like that," I commented sincerely.

"No. I would think not. Perhaps you will travel abroad during those months."

"That is an excellent idea."

We stood side by side, gazing out onto the ocean for a few moments without speaking.

"You've seen nothing of that Arthur Flett, I assume?" he said after a little while.

"No, but it's funny you mention him. My sister, Ingrid, was asking me about him just the other day."

"How so?"

"She was just confirming that I hadn't seen him after that last day at the castle. For some reason, she seemed particularly eager to be sure I hadn't forgotten anything."

"And had you?" Investigator Cairo asked.

"Why would I forget?"

"Oh, people forget all sorts of things, especially memories that are unpleasant. These events are frequently buried below consciousness."

"Consciousness?" I questioned.

He sighed and looked up pensively as though deciding how best to explain it. "I've been reading on the works of the German physician, Franz Mesmer. He put his patients in a trance state that enabled them to recall memories they had buried."

"How does one bury a memory?" I inquired. "Certainly not with a shovel."

He smiled. "Of course not."

"These unhappy memories can be locked away in the mind so that the person does not even recall that they ever occurred and is thus protected from the pain and fear caused by the event's memory," Investigator Cairo explained. "Dr. Mesmer is able to unlock those memories by a method that has come to be known as mesmerization."

"Thankfully I have none of those in my past," I said.

"You have never suffered a mental trauma?"

"Trauma?"

"An injury — in this case an injury to the mind. No assault on your psyche at all?"

I thought he was being overly personal and I didn't like it.

"Hasn't it been a mental trauma to you to never know your mother or your father?" Investigator Cairo asked.

"How do you know those things?" I asked, shocked and mildly offended at his impudence.

"I'm an investigator."

"I gather you don't think it rude to speak to someone you hardly know of personal matters such as that."

At this he smiled and shook his head wearily. "You must forgive me," he apologized. "My work as an investigator has sharpened my interest in everything to do with the workings of the human mind. I tend to ask questions that I consider professional, but others find boorish."

"I have never met someone who probed so deeply," I said.

"It is a passion of mine. I believe that someday there will be doctors who study nothing but the pathologies of the mind, the idea being that when people suffer from maladies of the mind they are alienated from their true selves. This alienation causes the afflicted person to behave in odd and even criminal ways."

"Interesting," I commented. "And do you believe that maladies of the mind are at the root of the current troubles in the area?"

"Some sort of madness is afoot," he said. "An Angus Martin who delivers dairy products around Gairsay has gone missing now. Do you know him?"

"Mrs. Flett takes care of all such things for us," I told him. But then I remembered an incident a few days earlier when I was walking alone and a man in a milk wagon had come up behind me so close that he startled me, causing me to stagger to my knees on the ground. The man came down from his wagon to help me, which would have been nice had he not been muttering angrily, extremely annoyed that I had been in his way.

After I told him about this, Investigator Cairo asked, "Were you injured?"

I held out my arms to show him where I was scraped and bruised from my fall, though modesty prevented me from showing him the bruises that were also on my knees.

"Those are bad," he said. "Have you seen a doctor?"

"I don't see the need. They'll heal. I'd rather just forget about it."

"There! You see?" he cried triumphantly.

"See what?"

"An unpleasant event pushed away under the carpet of forgetfulness."

"I could remember it if I wanted to," I argued. "I simply choose not to."

"You're right. It's not quite the same thing," he allowed.

We chatted about one thing and another until we reached Gairsay. Investigator Cairo helped me with the bags of things I'd purchased in Stromness as he escorted me back to the castle. "Would you mind if I came by one of these days for a call?" he asked at the door.

"Would it be business or pleasure?" I asked.

He thought about this for a moment before answering, "A bit of both."

CHAPTER TWENTY-NINE

FROM THE JOURNAL OF

INGRID VDW FRANKENSTEIN

August 17, 1815

Conscience. Shakespeare has Hamlet say it makes cowards of us all. Does it? That question has been on my mind a lot lately.

I think it does. Every time I stop to question my actions — the rightness or wrongness of them — I am thwarted in my resolve. I must stick to my one goal: to return Walter to his former health. The intense love I feel for him drives me. It is my only concern.

But it is a grisly business. If, before I began, I had truly comprehended the magnitude of the gore involved, it certainly would have sickened me into abandoning my plans. At the end of every day the white lab apron I wear is soaked in blood. Despite scrubbing in the laboratory sink, the skin on my hands is becoming tinged with red.

Poor Walter. He suffers so. For his own good, I keep him in a nearly perpetual state of deep intoxication. When he groans or stirs, I pour strong alcohol down his throat. He is becoming quite thin even though I mix mashed food in with the fluid in order to sustain him.

Thanks to our donor, he has a new right leg attached at the knee and a new right hand and forearm. It was much more arduous and time-consuming work than I had imagined, and I am afraid to miss even the tiniest detail. Joint bones must be filed to fit their new host. Tendons must be reattached. Muscles reconnected, nerves and veins allowed to find their paths.

Some of it is the work of a butcher. Other times I feel like a lace-maker tatting her delicate fibers with deft fingers.

It is tedious and wearying. I labor at it for hours and hours each day until I am close to collapse. At times I throw myself across my beloved's broad expanse of chest, sobbing with nervous exhaustion, wondering whether this quest I have embarked upon is madness itself. Am I a love-crazed lunatic who has lured poor dear Walter into an insanity of my own making? The solace of my love's barely thumping heart is all that consoles me and keeps me going.

And what of Riff? Are the sins of bravado, rudeness, and conceit really so dire that he deserved such an end — to be packed in ice and cut apart? When I am done, I will make a grave for him and throw what remains into the ground. I dare not mark it, though. Perhaps it will be safer to simply drop what's left in the ocean.

I think of all those cadavers I saw in the medical college. Didn't the college itself look the other way when it came to the unsavory methods of their procurement? Why must I struggle to do the same?

August 18

Giselle is aggravating me so, constantly clucking about this party next week. How can I care about it when I have so much on my mind?!

Walter's life hangs in the balance, entirely in my hands. I don't want to overstrain him, and with each new procedure I must give his body time to heal and recover. But at the same time I can't take too long. How much longer can Walter survive in this alcohol-induced half sleep?

The pressure is more than I can bear sometimes. Only sleep can mend my frayed nerves, and many nights sleep won't come. If only it would get truly dark! This continual daylight could drive anyone insane!

If Giselle doesn't stop nagging me, I will strangle her! She says my appearance is diminished from studying too much, and I won't look good when our guests arrive for the party!

The party!

Who cares? Who cares! Who cares about a stupid party?!

If she's not complaining that I am disinterested in her frivolous gala, then she is annoyed because I am not paying sufficient attention to her or Uncle Ernest — or the world around me, apparently.

Just minutes ago, she was berating me for this. "You are so involved in your studies that you don't even realize that there have been two more murders. Investigator Cairo has been coming by to report them to me."

"Who has been killed?" This shocking news *did* grab my attention.

"One was right here on the island — a worker was killed. And the other was in Stromness, not far from the dressmaker where I got our gowns." From there, she went on to scold me for not having tried on the gown she'd had made for me.

There are only two reasons I am eager for this party. Dr. Sarlandière is coming. Jakob Berzelius has also accepted. There are questions I need to ask them before I run electric current throughout Walter's body. For that reason — and that alone — I am counting the days until our guests arrive. Hopefully Dr. Berzelius will come earlier than the others, as he suggested he might.

August 19 (continued)

I have reached a most astonishing point in my father's riveting narrative. I can hardly pull myself from it. Having animated the man he has created, Victor Frankenstein finds that this man-creation has gone wildly out of his control. He torments my father. *He* is the nemesis that threatens all who my father loves. What cruel irony! His stalker is the thing he himself created.

As I continue to read my father's writings, I think I understand why he felt such revulsion toward the creation that he calls the Monster. It was his own ineptitude that caused the creature's deformity. Victor Frankenstein, who had figured out how to overcome death itself, could not lay in simple stitches as any beginning physician can. Perhaps it was his youth, or his haste, or his growing madness. If his creature had not been a human wreck of monstrous proportion, all the other misery that came after — which I am now breathlessly reading for the first time — might not have happened.

This reading of my father's tragic story fills me with caution. While I want to replace Walter's stiffening skin, at least on his face, I must not destroy his handsome face with a slip of my own quivering hand. And so, I hesitate. But this procrastination cannot go on indefinitely.

Tonight I will guard over my Walter, sitting beside his bed as usual, reading. Among the books Anthony lent me is one on the work of Sushruta, India's great ancient surgeon, who was repairing facial injuries incurred in battles in 600 B.C.

Before I begin to read, I must mention one last strange occurrence. The head I scooped from the sea and keep in a jar is changing. The skin is tightening and the film is dissolving from the eyes. Some quality in the preserving fluid must be causing this. I will keep a close watch.

He is stirring. I must attend to him. . . .

August 20

I read for hours and hours and hours until sleep overcame me right there in the chair where I sat. What a night of discovery!

Sushruta was fascinating. He burned mustard seeds to create cleansing fumes to soothe the nerves of the patient he was working on. He used boiled butter to clean wounds. But it was not Sushruta that kept me glued to my chair for hours.

I've learned why my father came here and what he was doing. It was all in the last of the three albums.

He had come here for the isolation of this barely populated island. His Monster had demanded a mate. In exchange, he would never bother my father again.

What a revelation! My father estranged himself from Giselle and me to save us from the Monster's vengeance.

My father got in touch with Gallagher. This time, the human he made from body parts was a female. And she was beautiful. But without intending to, he fashioned a woman who looked just like our mother.

In a fit of panic — and maybe of jealousy — he decided not to give the Monster this female who looked just like his dead wife. Instead, he dismembered her, sailed out to the middle of the ocean, and threw the parts overboard.

But what he didn't know was that the head would wash ashore, years later.

I have the head of Frankenstein's bride in a jar!

Even now I can see her gazing at me. Did this head really once look like my mother? I've seen small paintings of her. This, though, is so real.

I now know all my father learned in creating this newer, more refined version of the original creature. For one thing, he found a stronger, more delicate stitching thread. He had a supply of it somewhere here in the laboratory. He also learned to freeze the skin before stitching.

I have to stop writing because there is so much to do. I will begin by applying ice to Walter's face.

August 20 (continued)

It's done, and I'm afraid it has not turned out as cleanly as I had wished. There is swelling I hope will subside with time. The stitches show and both eyes are deeply purple underneath, as is the whole right half of his face.

It's monstrous.

I hate myself right now. This is exactly what I didn't want to happen. Exactly!

But bruises heal. Swelling goes down. I mustn't lose heart.

Walter stirred and I hurried to his side.

"My skin isn't hard," he slurred. His lip twitched in an attempt to smile, and that was encouraging. I hadn't killed the nerves in his face. "You did it," he whispered hoarsely.

"Sleep now," I told him, bringing the bottle of spirits to his lips. "Rest and heal." In a second he was sleeping once more.

I have no patience for this party tomorrow. I haven't even tried on my dress. I will have to steal away often to check on Walter. His health seems so fragile right now.

Tomorrow I will speak to the scholars at the party. (Anthony has written to say that his medical studies will keep him in Edinburgh.) If the scholars give me the answers I am hoping for, I will begin slowly introducing electric current section by section into Walter's body with the hope of reinvigorating the nerves.

As I write this, the head of Frankenstein's bride, the replica of my mother, seems to peer at me from the jar on the shelf. Do I see blame in her gaze?

Am I doing what my father before me did — creating a love for myself? When Victor Frankenstein realized what he had unwittingly done, he destroyed his work. But was that the right thing to do? What harm would there have been if he had let her live, loved her, and then made another mate for the Monster?

Walter moans in his sleep, and I brush away dark curls from his forehead.

By the end of this month, my Walter will be a new man. A man whom I will love always.

CHAPTER THIRTY

FROM THE DIARY OF

BARONESS GISELLE FRANKENSTEIN

August 20, 1815

Lord Byron was the first to arrive at the castle, and I would wager that he is possibly the most handsome man alive, and utterly charming too. I was happy to have just finished forming my last ringlet as I saw him strolling up the lane. I quickly ran down to greet him.

He was lavish in his praise of the castle and of me. "I decided to come because I was raised in Scotland and longed to see it once more, but the sight of your beauty is reward enough."

"You are too kind," I said as he kissed the silk of my elbow-high gloves.

"Your gown is perfection," he told me. "Paris or Milan?"

"Istanbul," I lied, caught up in the glamour of it all and hoping to impress such a worldly man. I immediately regretted it, because I saw skepticism in his appraisal. "The fabric, that is," I covered. "I had it made especially here in Scotland."

He gazed around at the dusky summer dim and smiled. "I would say that you walk in beauty like the night, except I see that there is no night to be found."

I would have talked the whole evening with him except that guests were arriving on each ferry, and I had to greet them all. The next to arrive were several of my former classmates from home. I asked my friend Margaret if there had been any news from Johann, and she said no one had heard anything. "His father is sick over this," she added. "He must have met with foul play. It's the only thing that would explain it."

The little orchestra that I had hired from Kirkwall took its place by the tall fireplace that I'd had lit for the party. They played some local ballads that were slow and melodic. The servants were all dressed formally and began to pass food on silver trays and to serve drinks from the side tables.

I came upon Percy Bysshe Shelley, whom I recognized from drawings in literary journals, though he seemed younger than I would have thought. He was standing by the musicians, gazing up at the portrait of my father. By his side was a slim, pretty woman who must not have been much older than me. When I introduced myself and welcomed him, he turned to the woman and made her known as "Mary, my wife."

"Who is this striking gentleman?" she asked, nodding up at the painting.

"He is my father, Victor Frankenstein, though he is deceased and this was painted some years ago."

"What fire in those eyes!" she remarked. "He fascinates me."

"This is a Copley, is it not?" Percy Shelley inquired.

"It is," I confirmed.

"I believe he's just arrived," he said, nodding toward the door at a tall, middle-aged man. I sensed Copley was a bit ill at ease, so I asked the Shelleys' pardon and went to his side. After we'd made introductions, and I'd reunited him with the painting, he told me he had painted my father in return for some medical care before he had achieved fame for his portraits.

"There is an exquisite quality to the light here on this island," Copley remarked. "Would it be an imposition if I stayed a day or two to paint?"

I assured him it would be wonderful. This was just what I wanted, a house alive with the fascinating and successful and interesting from all walks of life! Everything was going perfectly . . . but where was Ingrid? I had been so aggravated that she had simply disappeared this last week when I could have used her help. If she didn't show up at all now, I would be beyond furious!

Just when I was about to become enraged at her, I saw her standing in the center of a circle of scholars, their wives, and their assistants, all engaged in spirited conversation. Ingrid looked wonderful in the sapphire-blue gown, and she'd even put her hair up in coils at the top of her head. She was as avid in conversation as the rest of them, and I guessed they'd started talking on the ferry over and hadn't stopped.

For hours I greeted guests continuously, making sure no one ever lacked for a beverage or food. I was having a wonderful time, but it was exhausting and I wished Ingrid would be equally social to guests other than scholars. As the time passed, this resentment grew until I approached the cluster of scholars determined to draw Ingrid away for some assistance — only to discover that she was not there.

"Your sister is the most brilliant person, man or woman, that I have ever met," said a man in his late twenties who introduced himself as Dr. Jean-Baptiste Sarlandière. "We have learned so much from each other just now."

"Do you know where she went?" I asked.

He pointed toward the front door. "We were discussing the fine points of electrotherapy when she suddenly remembered something urgent she had to do and dashed off. I do hope she will return to resume our discussion."

"She went out the door, you say?" I was incensed! How dare she abandon me in the middle of the most important event of my life!

I hurried outside, where guests were spread out on the lawn, all chatting amiably. Had she gone off to find Walter or to get back to her studies? Either way, I would drag her back no matter what it took.

Hurrying out to the cliff, I saw it was just as I had suspected: She was in the rowboat crossing over to Sweyn Holm. She was rowing in her gown!

And now she had the boat so I couldn't even cross over and find her to demand that she return. I was furious!

I could always get there through the tunnel . . . if only I had the nerve. I would get lamps. I'd get others to come with me, so there would be no danger.

Ingrid had abandoned me all these weeks and I would put up with it no more!

As I headed back into the house, I literally ran into Investigator Cairo.

"Fräulein Frankenstein," he said, "please forgive me for coming. I did not know you were having an event."

"Not at all, Investigator. Please eat and drink. Enjoy yourself. If you'll excuse me, I have urgent business."

I was not going to be deterred by anyone or anything.

Ingrid was going to come back to the party.

CHAPTER THIRTY-ONE

FROM THE JOURNAL OF

INGRID VDW FRANKENSTEIN

August 20, 1815

"If one could run current over a body within twenty-four hours of the last transplant, I believe that the creation would be strong and disease-free," Dr. Sarlandière told me. "I am sure of it." We had been discussing curing sickness with electricity. He seemed so brilliant that I couldn't doubt anything he said.

"It's highly experimental, but I believe you are correct," agreed the portly Dr. Berzelius, speaking in heavily accented English.

That was when I fled from the party. If he was right, I had two hours to work with Walter. If I got it right, he would be healthy and strong forever.

Climbing down the ladder was not easy in the long gown. The minute I reached the bottom, I pulled the dress off, tossing it away, and put a white apron on over my chemise. I hurried to Walter's side, throwing aside his blanket.

He did not stir as he usually did.

Frightened, I grabbed his wrist and did not feel a pulse. I laid my head on his heart but heard no beat. There was no breath on my hand. He was very cold.

"Walter!" I shouted. "Walter!" My frenzied voice climbed to a shriek. "Walter!"

I paced in circles. I'd killed Walter. I'd killed him. Reckless. Murderous. Arrogant. Mad. I'd killed Walter. My love! My love! My love!

I started moving very fast, although everything seemed dreamlike. I covered him in wires and receptors. I activated my two battery drums. The current moved back and forth slowly at first.

"I need more," I mumbled, frustrated. The frequency increased somewhat. "More!" I screamed at it. "More!" As if it had heard me, there was a further increase. The battery crackled with energy.

Walter wasn't moving, though. Nothing was happening.

"Walter, don't die! Wake up!"

It was no use. He didn't stir. I let the current run until I smelled burning flesh and hair. Char marks began to form across his forehead.

"Ingrid, what is all this?" I whirled toward Giselle's voice. She stood only yards away with an oil lantern in her hand. Behind her were Lord Byron, Percy Shelley, and Mary Shelley, all with lanterns.

"Our father's laboratory. I would have told you but I wanted —"

I was cut short by a sharp gasp from Mary Shelley. Her eyes were wide and she was pointing a trembling hand at something behind me. Turning, I clapped my hand over my mouth in shock.

Walter was sitting up.

His face was swollen and his eyes blackened. His jaw jutted at an odd angle and the char marks streaked his forehead. His black curls were frayed and burned. He was speechless, dazed.

Giselle coughed and started shifting from foot to foot. Her eyes were wild with fear. Then she strode up to Walter and was suddenly wielding a scalpel she'd snapped up from my instrument table.

"You won't get me this time, fiend!" she screamed, plunging the scalpel into his stomach. "I'll kill you! I'll kill you first!"

Lord Byron and Percy Shelley quickly grabbed Giselle while I stuffed gauze into Walter's wound. Mary Shelley raced back into the tunnel to the castle.

I had no idea what she would do. Would she tell the others? Reveal what she had seen to our guests? I was kept busy staunching the blood gushing from Walter's wound. He writhed in pain that was awful to see. But amid this torture a movement of his caught my attention. He was clenching and unclenching his hand — his *right* hand!

Oh, what joy tangled into this moment of frenzied fear!

His right hand moved. It worked!

My elation was quickly thwarted as Walter fainted back onto the table. With my head to his chest, I listened frantically to find a heartbeat. I thought I heard something but maybe it was only the gurgle of blood in his veins. It was hard to tell.

Percy and Byron continued struggling with Giselle, who squirmed and arched as she endeavored to free herself from their grip. The two men were young and strong, but it was as though her terror had imbued her with a supernatural strength. She struggled and screamed as if in a nightmare from which she couldn't awaken.

"Giselle, be calm," I tried to soothe her as I pounded Walter's chest, hoping to get his heart going. "It's me, Ingrid."

"Ingrid, run to the house. Get Grandfather. Hurry!" Her voice sounded young as she implored me. It was as I recalled it from childhood.

"Why did you attack Walter?" I asked. "What has he ever done to you?"

"He's the bad man. He wants to take us. He can't take us."

"She's out of her mind," Lord Byron remarked.

"Totally mad," Percy Shelley agreed.

Giselle struggled fiercely, almost escaping their grip. "HE CAN'T TAKE US!"

Just then Mary Shelley returned with Dr. Sarlandière, who had brought his medical bag. He came from behind and covered Giselle's nose with a handkerchief. It calmed her immediately. He handed the handkerchief to Lord Byron.

"It's only laudanum," the doctor explained. "Put it over her nose when she gets upset. You should probably get her upstairs."

Lord Byron and Percy Shelley propped Giselle between them and walked her toward the stairway, with Mary Shelley right behind.

"Get our uncle," I said. "I must not leave Walter."

I turned to Dr. Sarlandière, who was checking Walter's heartbeat by holding his wrist. "The pulse is faint but it exists."

What relief!

"Will he live?" I asked.

"You've been experimenting on him, haven't you?"

"I wanted to cure him," I admitted.

"You might have."

"What do you mean?" I asked, suddenly hopeful.

"I can see you've replaced his right leg and hand with exquisite skill. You've done an excellent job of grafting new skin to his face."

"Thank you." I was so pleased at this. "I have to confess that one reason I had my sister invite you was to learn from your genius. What must I do next to bring him to health? He has a disease of the nerves. Can you tell me your opinion?"

"I observe that this man has one or multiple sclerosis diseases. I can tell it simply by looking at him. He also shows signs of having had systemic sclerosis scleroderma. Dr. Carlo Curzio wrote a fascinating paper on it in seventeen fifty-five. It accounts for the patches of hard skin."

"Signs of *having had*," I echoed, growing frightened again. He'd never told me if Walter would live.

"As I said, you might have cured him as you intended. The scorch marks tell me you have run high voltage through this man, enough to kill him, though thankfully he still lives. The concept is the same as what I have been attempting with more caution in my own work. You have made a reckless experiment, but now that it is done, let's see what happens."

I was filled with new hope.

"The patient now has a stab wound to contend with on top of everything else. If you'll allow me, I'll stay and work on him."

"You will?" I cried, filled with gratitude.

"This is a fascinating opportunity for me. I even brought my acupuncture needles." He checked Walter, then turned back to me. "I'll stay here with him. You'd better go to your sister."

When I reached my twin, she was slumped between Uncle Ernest and Investigator Cairo on the front lawn. All the guests had moved inside.

"I'm taking her into custody," Investigator Cairo told me. "I came here tonight to arrest her."

"For what?" I cried.

"For the murder of Johann Gottlieb. But I suspect she is also guilty of murdering Captain Fynn Ramsay, your dairyman, and a man in Stromness named Kyle MacNab. I'm still working on the disappearance of Arthur Flett, but I'm pretty sure it will trace back to Giselle in the end."

"What motive would she have for killing these people?" I challenged.

"Ever hear of a condition called hysteria?" Investigator Cairo asked.

I shook my head.

"Sometimes upsetting, only partially remembered events in a person's life set off a series of symptoms. Some patients have seizures, partial paralysis, and sometimes even temporary blindness. My guess is that certain triggers send Giselle back in time to a disturbing event. She might feel like she's fighting for her life over and over again."

"How awful for her," I said. Of course I knew he was right. I had seen it for myself earlier. Poor Giselle! What had frightened her so deeply that it had caused such disturbance in her mind?

In minutes I had thrown on my plain gray dress and joined Investigator Cairo and Uncle Ernest again. I had to believe Dr. Sarlandière would be best alone with Walter. Now I had to help my sister.

Leaving behind a castle ablaze in light and the curious conversation of guests, I went off to accompany Giselle to jail.

CHAPTER THIRTY-TWO

FROM THE DIARY OF

BARONESS GISELLE FRANKENSTEIN

Glasgow, Scotland
November 1815

So, Diary, it's another day with the nuns here at the women's home for the mentally unstable. I am awaiting trial for five alleged murders — which is impossible! I couldn't have killed these men. Investigator Cairo has petitioned for more time so it can be proven that I am not mentally fit.

How humiliating either way they present it: Either I'm a fiend or a lunatic.

I am told they kept me on this drug called laudanum for weeks while they waited to transfer me here. Once here, they have weaned me from it. At first Ingrid and Investigator Cairo stayed with me and tried to question me, inquiring why I had murdered five men. I didn't know why they were asking such a ridiculous question. Murdered?! What an insane question; clearly it was they who were acting crazy. I would never murder anyone!

After my second week, Investigator Cairo came to visit me accompanied by Ingrid and a Frenchman he introduced as the Marquis de Puységur. He was thick-featured with hooded eyes, yet I found his accent and his manner charming. "They tell me, mademoiselle, that you walk in your sleep," he said, taking my hand gently.

"Yes. I have been known to walk in my sleep," I confirmed.

"She hasn't done it in over a month," Ingrid added, laying on my bed table the fresh linens and nightgowns she brings me every week without fail.

"The marquis was a student of Franz Mesmer, who died this past March. Marquis de Puységur is his foremost follower and renowned in his own form of mesmerization, which he calls artificial somnambulance."

"I will induce a state in you that will be much the same as the waking dream of one who walks while asleep," de Puységur explained. "That way I will be able to plumb the inner workings of your mind."

This worried me. "And what do you hope to find in the depths of my mind?" I asked cautiously.

"Memories — deep and long-forgotten memories."

I didn't like this one bit and turned away from them. "I don't want to."

"It is painless," the marquis prodded.

"Please, Giselle. Perhaps it will help prove your innocence," Investigator Cairo added.

"I think you should try it," Ingrid urged.

I studied them both warily, unsure of what to believe. As it turned out I should never have let them persuade me because the outcome was shockingly disastrous.

I have pasted the confession I allegedly made under the influence of this artificial somnambulance here using sealing wax. It is written in Investigator Cairo's handwriting since he claims to have transcribed my every word, and I still doubt its truth as it is too amazing to be real.

The first time that the bad man came to get me was when I was six. Ingrid and I were in our beds in our room by the garden on the first floor. I opened my eyes and there he was, looking in the long window. I could see his face because the moon was very bright. It was a monster's face, scarred with bulging eyes and gray-green skin.

I screamed when he punched in the window and crashed his way in. He grabbed Ingrid and me from our beds, carrying each of us in one hand. I beat his shoulders and face, kicked at him, but he was too strong. Ingrid was so scared, she couldn't do anything but look at him with giant frightened eyes.

He took us into the garden and Grandfather came out with his rifle. When he shot into the air, shouting for the horrible creature to release us, the Monster got scared and dropped us. He ran away into the night.

Have I ever seen him again?

He didn't come back for a long time. We were safe with our grandfather because he had a rifle. But then we made the mistake of leaving Grandfather and the bad man came after us.

The next time I saw him was in a park in Edinburgh. He grabbed me and knocked me down. Lucky for me there was a rock nearby. I pounded him in the head until he stopped struggling, and then I rolled him in a nearby river.

He then tried to drown me in Millburn Bay, but I saw through his disguise as the captain of a boat. His piercing, hate-filled eyes gave him away. He whispered evil things to me, and I knew as soon as he had the chance he would try to kill me. When he sailed into a hidden bay where no one could see him strike, I knew it would be a fight to the death. He capsized the boat and would soon kill me if I hadn't acted boldly and wrapped the sailing line around his neck.

I thought I had stopped him but somehow he got out and followed me back to the castle where I live in Gairsay. I was in an underground tunnel waiting for Ingrid when he grabbed me in the dark. I fought with him and smashed my lantern. I stabbed him with a jagged piece of glass and got away.

He wanted to attack me again on a street in Stromness, but this time he pretended to be sweet. He asked me to join him in a pub but I knew what he really wanted — a chance to get me alone to murder me. Luckily I spied rat poison in the kitchen and was able to slip inside to grab some. While he tried to woo me with sweet words I slipped it into his ale, thereby making my escape. He followed me into the alley but as the first convulsions suddenly overtook him, I dashed away.

It wasn't long, though, before the monstrously invincible creature was after me once more. He made his way to Gairsay where he tried again as I walked home, only this time he was in a wagon and got out to kidnap me. Fortunately I possessed a letter opener, which I used to fight him off.

The last time I saw him he was sitting up on a bed in a hospital or somewhere like it. I'm not sure what it was. Ingrid was there and he was attacking her this time. I saved both of us that day.

Since I've been here I haven't seen him. But if I do see him, I won't let him get me or Ingrid. I'll protect us.

I don't remember saying any of this: Clearly the effects of artificial somnambulance put me into a nightmare state where my mind concocted a nightmare vista where I played the role of . . . Of what? Brave heroine? Deluded dreamer? Mad murderess?

I awoke screaming frantically. Ingrid and Investigator Cairo tried to soothe me, but the fear that this induced dream brought to me was unbearable. My mind felt it would explode with the terror of it all. Nothing but the laudanum would calm me, and I have been dosed with it ever since.

The marquis came again today wanting to put me in a trance state once again. He says he wants me to remember the incident of the Monster trying to kidnap us when we were little, but I don't want to remember anything. Maybe some things are just too terrifying to think about. I still say, some truths are better left unexplored.

EPILOGUE

FROM THE JOURNAL OF

INGRID VDW FRANKENSTEIN

December 1815

I am sitting now by the big fire with the portrait of my father gazing down on me. The days have grown very short and I long for the summer of endless sunlight. Life is very quiet at the castle with Giselle in Glasgow. It is lonely and I miss her more than I can say, though I visit as often as I can.

I am happy to say that with Dr. Sarlandière's help, things went very well with Walter. He still needs a cane, but he's walking. He has regained the use of his right hand as well. His face, though scarred, I still find handsome. I like the character his imperfections have imparted. He still suffers from bouts of melancholia, but I hope that as he gets stronger, those will improve. He is deeply grateful and we remain close, though he still insists it would be too selfish of him to ask me to share my life with him as his wife. Still . . . maybe . . . with time. Time and my continued scientific efforts on his behalf. I dream of Walter in all his former glory, healthy and in love with me.

Often I think about the things Giselle said when she was giving her confession. Surely the man who came to snatch us from our beds that night was the Monster that Victor Frankenstein created, once more seeking his endless revenge on my father. Do I remember the incident?

I have searched my brain and simply can't dredge it up. It's one of the mysteries of the mind. Why one person is destroyed by the same event that another — and a twin at that — is fortunate enough to survive?

But just tonight I experienced a glimmer of a memory as I gazed out the front window. The moon was bright and I saw the hunched and lopsided form of an extremely large man silhouetted in its glow.

I shuddered and turned away. When I looked back, it was gone.

AUTHOR'S NOTE

Clearly I owe a huge debt to Mary Shelley's gothic masterpiece *Frankenstein* and have done my best to honor it, though in several places I have taken creative license with the story. In the original novel, Victor Frankenstein was nineteen when he brought his Monster to life. (Shelley herself was eighteen when she wrote the first draft and twenty-one when the first edition was published anonymously in London in 1818.) His family is unaware of his life at the University of Ingolstadt, and I thought it plausible that he might have married and had twin babies during that time, though this is a fiction of my own making and does not derive from the original novel. His pursuit by and the murderous intentions of his Creature are true to the original novel, as is his final demise in the Arctic Circle.

In the original *Frankenstein*, the Monster does demand a bride and Victor goes to Orkney to create that bride. I picked the island of Gairsay in the Orkney island chain partly because it is sparsely populated (a census of 1851 claimed that only six families lived there) and because it has a small island nearby of red sandstone named Sweyn Holm thought to be named after the Viking Sweyn Asleifsson. (How could I resist the name Sweyn?!) The Viking marauder built a castle there, which was later leveled and replaced by another in the 1600s. My Castle Frankenstein is fictitious. In the original, Victor Frankenstein simply works in a homemade laboratory on an uninhabited island in Orkney.

I have tried to be faithful to the science of the day, not even using the term scientist because my copyeditor, Annie McDonnell, diligently pointed out that it was not in use in 1815 (along with the other anachronistic words not used in 1815 that she took out of the manuscript). I fudged a little in one place and that is with Dr. Jean-Baptiste Sarlandière. This brilliant young French doctor from a family of doctors was born in 1787. He began his medical studies at the age of 16 and — after an eleven-year military career — received his medical degree in 1815 at the age of 28. He didn't publish his book on electroacupuncture until 1825 (*Mémoires sur l'electropuncture*), but I think it is plausible that he might have been thinking of it and experimenting years before publication, though this is only my own supposition, and so his appearance in this novel might be somewhat anachronistic. (But only somewhat, since he was a known figure on the cutting edge of the scientific scene in 1815.)

Lord Byron, Percy Shelley and, indeed, Mary Shelley — among other real historical luminaries mentioned — never attended a big party at the fictitious Castle Frankenstein on the very real island of Gairsay. They never saw the fictitious Walter Hammersmith being operated on in a laboratory on the real Sweyn Holm.

But what fun, if they had!

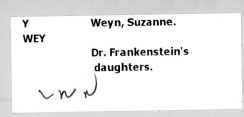